LAW RIDES THE RANGE

Wade Morgan killed the town boss in a vicious gun-fight and knew that he must make tracks—fast.

But he left his son Joe behind to make sure he got a fair deal.

What he didn't reckon with, though, was the terrible revenge that Bull Mitchell's renegade crew decided to take—a terrifying act of retribution that brought Wade Morgan back to town with a smoking gun and a heart full of hate. . .

Walt Coburn was born in White Sulphur Springs, Montana Territory. He was once called "King of the Pulps" by Fred Gipson and promoted by Fiction House as "The Cowboy Author". He was the son of cattleman Robert Coburn, then owner of the Circle C ranch on Beaver Creek within sight of the Little Rockies. Coburn's family eventually moved to San Diego while still operating the Circle C. Robert Coburn used to commute between Montana and California by train and he would take his youngest son with him. When Coburn got drunk one night, he had an argument with his father that led to his leaving the family. In the course of his wanderings he entered Mexico and for a brief period actually became an enlisted man in the so-called "Gringo Battalion" of Pancho Villa's army.

Following his enlistment in the U.S. Army during the Great War, Coburn began writing Western short stories. For a year and a half he wrote and wrote before selling his first story to Bob Davis, editor of *Argosy-All Story*. Coburn married and moved to Tucson because his wife suffered from a respiratory condition. In a little adobe hut behind the main house Coburn practiced his art and for almost four decades he wrote approximately 600,000 words a year. Coburn's early fiction from his Golden Age – 1924–1940 – is his best, including his novels, *Mavericks* (1929) and *Barb Wire* (1931), as well as many short novels published only in magazines that now are being collected for the first time. In his Western stories, as Charles M. Russell and Eugene Manlove Rhodes, two men Coburn had known and admired in life, he captured the cow country and recreated it just as it was already passing from sight.

LAW RIDES THE RANGE

Walt Coburn

GUNSMOKE

This hardback edition 2001
by Chivers Press
by arrangement with
Golden West Literary Agency

Copyright © 1935 by Walt Coburn
Copyright © renewed 1963 by Walt Coburn

ISBN 0 7540 8137 0

British Library Cataloguing in Publication Data available

Printed and bound in Great Britain by
Bookcraft, Midsomer Norton, Somerset

Chapter One

"OUTLAWED"

I RECKON," said Wade Morgan, and he spoke without looking up from the headstall he was making, "that I'll have to kill Shotgun Riley."

Long Bob Burch, Wade's partner in the cow business, laid down a copy of the *Drovers' Journal*. His big, square-jawed, handsome face showed no surprise. His eyes, dark and opaque and unfathomable, studied Wade's bent head. Wade looked up and smiled. It was a boy's smile, and it softened the expression of a face that was becoming a little too grim.

"Better think 'er over careful, Wade. Yuh know what it means."

Wade's smile hardened and became a crooked line. His hazel eyes changed expression.

"I've done thought 'er all out, Bob. Shotgun Riley has made his talk. He's out to either gut-shoot me or run me outa the country like I was a damn coyote. So, before I quit this country, I'm goin' into town and kill Shotgun." He again bent to his work on the headstall.

From the kitchen came the sounds of dishes being washed. A woman's voice hummed the gay little tune of a song. A small boy's laugh came from outside. Long Bob scowled thoughtfully —because the woman was Hattie Morgan, common-law wife of Wade Morgan. The boy was their son, Joe. Long Bob always called the youngster "Little Britches."

"What about Hattie and the young 'un, Wade?"

"I got that figgered out, too. You'll take care of 'em, Bob?"

"Better all around, Wade, if I took care uh Shotgun Riley."

Wade Morgan looked up, his face red under the layers of tan.

"And have folks say that I didn't have the guts to take up my own fight? Every white man, breed, and Injun in this section of Montana knows what Shotgun done to me. How he threw down on me with a gun, called me every dirty name he could lay his tongue on, laughed at me, and told me he'd make a bunch quitter outa me. Said he'd take a rope and whup me outa the country because I was a cow thief and a coward. He did that in his saloon with his friends backin' his play. Bull Mitchell, his pardner, stood behind me. Made me take it. Hattie and Joe was outside in the buckboard waitin' for me.

She heard part of it. The part that called her a bad woman. He said that little Joe was just a bastard. And they was hopin, I'd make a break so they could kill me. . . . It's my fight, Bob. I'm killin' Shotgun Riley."

"Said anything to Hattie?"

"Not yet, but I reckon she knows it's in my craw. She's game enough to take it standin' up. You'll look after her and Joe when I'm gone? I'll send money."

"To hell with the money."

"Yo're the one man I call friend, Bob." Wade Morgan tossed the finished headstall on the table and got to his feet.

"I'll pull out for town in about half an hour, Bob. Might as well get it done and over with."

He went into the kitchen. Long Bob went outside and over to the log barn. Little Joe spied him and came after him, riding a stick horse, some lubberly hound pups at his small heels.

The boy, ten years old, looked like his father. Black curly hair, hazel eyes that looked straight into the eyes of any one, a straight nose and square little jaw. A quick smile that was like a flicker of sunshine across a gray sky. His bones were small, his movements quick and smooth.

"H'lo there, Little Britches. Travelin' er a-goin' somewhere? I see you're ridin' a mare."

"That's a darn lie. Nobody but sheepherders ride mares. I ain't any sheepherder and you know it."

"Doggone. I shore made a mistake. Eyes must be a-goin' back on me. I'd uh swore that was wool a-stickin' outa yore ears."

Little Britches watched Long Bob saddle his horse. "Goin' to town, Bob?"

"I reckon."

"Will you fetch me back some BB shot for my air-gun?"

"I reckon." Long Bob shoved a carbine into the saddle scabbard.

Wade was coming from the kitchen. Around his middle was a double-rowed cartridge belt. The holster that held a Colt .45 was tied down. He carried a Winchester carbine in the crook of his arm. A little under medium height, he walked with a quick, springy step. His shoulders were wide and powerful, his waist without an ounce of fat, his flanks were narrow. Wade Morgan had no fear of any man. He was one of the best riders in the Northwest—a crack shot and a top cowhand.

Under the gray Stetson, his face was grim looking, twisted with grief. He stooped and gathered up Joe, trying to cover the ache in his heart with a grin.

"I'm goin' away for a spell, Joe." His voice was husky. "Be a good kid and look after yore mother. You better trot over to the house. She don't feel very good."

Another man would have kissed the boy. But Wade Morgan had never known how to be demonstrative. Any display of emotion embarrassed him. He set the boy down and Joe, riding his stick horse, went back to the house.

"You ridin' with me a ways, Bob? asked Wade Morgan as he saddled a powerful black gelding.

"All the way, Wade. I'm aimin' tuh see you git a fair break."

The two men rode away together. Hattie Morgan, standing at the front window, watched them out of sight. Her soft brown eyes were blurred with tears. She clung tightly to Joe's soiled little hands. Her heart felt like a lump of cold lead.

The two riders topped a ridge and were lost to sight.

With dragging steps Hattie Morgan went back to her panful of dishes. Hers was that splendid courage that had been her mother's, a pioneer woman who had driven an ox-team across the plains. Little Joe washed his hands clean and found a dish-towel. There was a lump in his throat. Somehow the small boy knew that something was wrong. He had heard the cowpunchers at the bunkhouse talking about Shotgun Riley and Bull Mitchell. He had listened, as only a small boy can listen, with a boy's understanding.

"I bet," he told his mother, "that Dad and Long Bob are goin' to town to kill Shotgun Riley. Shotgun Riley is a damn skunk and if Dad don't git him first, he'll git Dad and he'll git 'im where his galluses cross."

"Who's been filling you full of such things?" his mother asked.

"I saw Almanac Jones bet that bronc stomper from the Long-X a bottle of whisky that Dad'd git Shotgun."

Hattie Morgan kept silent. But Joe went on.

"Almanac told 'em that if Dad ever turned bad, he'd go plumb bad. He said Wade Morgan would make some of these hen-yard sheriffs hard to ketch. Almanac said Dad could join the Wild Bunch any day he wanted. He said Dad had worked with Kid Curry and Butch Cassidy and the Sun Dance Kid. Almanac said that he bet—"

"Almanac," said Hattie Morgan, "talks too much with his mouth. And Dad or Bob won't thank you for talking a lot, either, sonny."

Silenced Joe. The habit of not talking gossip was among the lessons Wade had taught his son. A good cowpuncher keeps his mouth shut and tends to his own business. Almanac Jones was a grizzled old trail boss who was too knotted with broken, rheumatic bones to follow the strenuous work of the round-ups. He took care of the stable and puttered in the garden and called himself one of the family. He liked to talk and got drunk just as often as opportunity came his way. He wore an old bone-handled .45 as naturally as he wore boots or overalls or a hat. His blue eyes were bright and full of humor. His leathery face was seamed, fringed with white beard. And while no Montana man had ever seen that white-handled gun in action, it was a known fact that Jones was not his real name and that he had been in two big cattle wars in New Mexico and Texas. Because he read everything he could find, and was fond of using large words, because he was always quoting strange facts gleaned from numerous periodicals, they called him Almanac. To him, Hattie Morgan was an angel set down by God in the cow country. There was no doubting the fact that he would readily die to protect her or little Joe. Some said he was Wade Morgan's uncle and that after Wade's mother died and his father was killed in the Lincoln County War, Almanac Jones had taken the boy Wade and raised him.

Almanac Jones hobbled into the kitchen with a gunnysack half full of garden truck. His keen blue eyes looked at Hattie.

"Didn't I see Wade and Bob ride off?" he asked.

"Yes." Her voice was low but steady.

"They went to town?"

Hattie Morgan nodded. Almanac turned to Joe.

"Lope on down to the garden, Little Britches, and see if I dropped my pipe there along the irrigatin' ditch."

When the boy was gone, the old trail boss led her into the front room. He patted her hand as they sat down on the old-fashioned sofa.

"I knowed he had it on his mind. And once he starts, he'll play his string out. He'll kill Shotgun and kill him fair, but Bull Mitchell and their damned money would send Wade over the road. Or he'd git shot in the back some night. I knowed it was a-comin'. He's like his father. Prideful and hot blooded. Born doomed he was, Hattie, and I've knowed it. I've watched it grow in him—whatever it is that the devil puts into a man to make a killer out of him. His father was a killer and a bad 'un, and he's another. It's in the blood and it won't come out. After he kills Shotgun, he'll travel hard and he'll travel far, and there'll be a-plenty more human blood spattered along his trail. Doomed, by God, and mebby so Joe will foller the same trail, though he has a lot of yore blood in him. There is a destiny that points out the trail ahead.

"There was a spell when I hoped that his love for you would tame him. But it didn't. I'd read in books where men like him have been influenced by a good woman. I could tell them writers that they are all wrong. Wrong. I've done my best to talk it out of him, but it was in his blood like a disease. He was bound to go like he went to-day.

"It hurts now, Hattie, but after he's gone the months and years will heal the hurt like time crusts over a wound, and each year the scar will show dimmer. You'll have me here, and Bob, and there'll be little Joe. All of us will be missin' Wade. The hurt and lonesomeness will pull us closer together. When I die off, Bob Burch will look after yuh. Bob's a good man. I reckon he's the squarest man I ever knowed, bar none. Many's the poor devil on the dodge that Bob Burch has helped. And there ain't a man in the country, sheriffs, judges, preachers, that don't respect Bob's word. He's a good man, Hattie."

Hattie Morgan, sobbing softly against the faded old flannel shirt, nodded without lifting her face. She was thinking of what Wade Morgan had said before he left.

"I'm goin' yonderly, Hattie. I'm glad we was never married because when I'm gone I want you to marry Bob Burch. God only made one of his kind. He used up all the real material he had when he put it into Bob. I know you like him, Hattie. And I know that Bob thinks more of you than any woman on earth. He'll be good to you and Joe. Better than I've been, because he's a better man. I'll have a talk with him. Mebby I'll come back some day and visit yuh-all. So-long, Hattie. I'm driftin' yonderly."

Chapter Two

MAN FROM CHINOOK

IT WAS long past dark when Long Bob Burch got back to the ranch. He put up his horse and walked slowly toward the house where a lamp burned in the front room. Hattie and Almanac Jones were sitting there. Bob put his Winchester up in the gun rack and unbuckled his belt. He transferred his .45 from its holster to the waistband of his overalls and sat down facing them. His big, handsome face looked tired and a little old.

"Wade got 'im," he said quietly. "He give Shotgun a fair chance and shot him there in his own saloon. I kep' Mitchell and the rest of 'em from hornin' in. When Shotgun dropped, thumbin' his gun hammer, it kinda wilted his gang. They acted

9

like sheep. We got our horses and nobody tried to stop us when we pulled out. Wade's gone to join the Wild Bunch."

"Was Wade hurt?" asked Hattie Morgan. Her face looked white. Hattie Morgan was the prettiest girl in that section of the cow country. She had been raised on a ranch and was hard-muscled and slim as a boy. Her gray eyes and ash-colored hair made a striking contrast to her tanned skin. She had run off with Wade twelve years ago from her father's ranch on the Marias.

It was Almanac Jones who prevented a gun fight when her father rode up one day with a Winchester across his saddle and called Wade out of the house. The old man had returned home without his rifle. It was still up there in the rack. Uncalled for. Twelve years.

"No, Wade never got a scratch. Shotgun's two bullets clipped his hat. A man had always ought to shoot for the briskit. . . . Wade's three slugs ketched Shotgun in the chest and belly. He died a-cussin', slobberin' blood and tobacco juice, tryin' tuh pull back the hammer of his gun. He was a tough 'un."

There followed a silence. Long Bob was the one to break it.

"Wade said to tell you so-long for him, Almanac. He had some idee you'd try to keep him from killin' Shotgun, so he went off without shakin' hands."

Almanac Jones nodded, puffing hard on his pipe. There was another long silence. After a time they all three went to their beds to lie awake thinking of Wade Morgan who had killed a man and ridden away to join the Wild Bunch. Most probably they would never see him again. He would ride that dim outlaw trail that twisted its mysterious way from Montana to the Mexican line. Wade Morgan would have no home save those lawless spots such as the Hole-in-the-Wall, Robbers' Roost, and the Hideaway. He would be like some snarling, snapping wolf. Sometimes he would stay at a log cabin hidden in the bad-lands —a cabin whose logs bore the carved initials of men, dead and living, who had followed the trail. He would listen to the strange tales of men on whose heads the law put a price. There would be lonely campfires and the "Cowboy's Lament." There would be whisky and gambling and women with red slippers and painted faces. And in the end there would be death by bullet or a hangman's rope.

Almanac Jones knew. Long Bob knew. And because Hattie had lived all her life among cowpunchers, she also knew. Only Little Joe Morgan, whom Long Bob liked to call Little Britches, did not know what lay ahead to mark his father's chosen trail. Joe was too young to understand, just then. Later, years later, he

10

was to understand the way of the outlaw trail with all its blood and powder smoke and grief and defiance.

Joe's first bit of learning was given him the next day when a sheriff and a posse of a hundred men rode into the ranch. Joe and his mother stayed in the front room while Long Bob and old Almanac Jones met the sheriff and his men outside. Bull Mitchell and three of Shotgun Riley's gunmen were in the posse.

The sheriff was a pompous man with a belly that sagged like a sack of meal down over the lacing of his black angora chaps. Short-statured, heavy-shouldered, with restless black eyes. He had the reputation of being a killer, a bounty collector. A damn hide hunter, some called him. Shotgun Riley and Bull Mitchell had helped put him in office. His name was Sim Patchen.

"We're after Wade Morgan." His heavy voice carried to the woman and boy inside the house.

"So I reckon, Patchen," replied Long Bob in his soft-toned, drawling manner. Both Long Bob and Almanac Jones were armed. "You reckon yuh'll ever ketch up with him?"

"We're gonna search the ranch. Don't try tuh stop us, Burch, or there'll be trouble."

"Search yore damn heads off," said Long Bob. "But don't let any of that two-bit posse steal anything or hurt Hattie Morgan or the boy."

Long Bob and Almanac Jones accompanied the sheriff, two deputies, and Bull Mitchell when they went into the house. Hattie stood by the big sofa in the front room, little Joe by her side. The boy's eyes were wide with excitement.

"Did your father come home last night, young feller?" Sim Patchen asked.

"I don't talk with my mouth," said little Joe stoutly. Long Bob grinned. "You are after my Dad," Joe went on, "but I bet if he was to pop out, you'd run like a damn coyote."

Almanac Jones snickered. The sheriff got red in the face.

"Wise young brat you got," he told Hattie. "He'll hang some day."

"Did yuh look in the sugar bowl and see if we'd hid Wade there?" grinned Long Bob. " 'Er in the stove?"

Sim Patchen swung about, his temper on edge. "Better hold your tongue between your teeth, Bob Burch. You was with Morgan when he murdered Riley. You held off Mitchell and the others while Wade Morgan shot him down in cold blood. I may git out a warrant for yuh. You keep your gab shut."

"Gosh, you shore do scare me, Patchen, somethin' terrible. Dunno when I bin so scared."

The sheriff and his men went outside. They spent several

hours riding around the ranch, always in bunches of eight or ten, with their guns in their hands. When their mess-wagon caught up, Sim Patchen camped it on a creek a mile below the horse pasture. The cook was drunk. They were short of salt and Patchen wanted to buy some from Long Bob.

"We ain't runnin' a store," Bob told him. "And if I was, I'd be plumb outa salt."

"I'm butchering one of your steers for beef, Burch. I'll give you an order on the county."

"You won't butcher no steer of mine, Patchen. Not at any price. Show me where you got a right to destroy my property. Yo're breakin' the law a-comin' in here without a search warrant. You'll be in shore hot water if you shoot a beef of mine. That goes as she lays. I got a right to protect my property. I'm doin' it with a Winchester. I'll kill the man that kills a steer of mine or ropes a horse wearin' my iron. And there ain't a law in the country that can touch me. Now take yore posse and move on. I'm a-goin' down in the field directly, me and Almanac Jones. Coyotes and bear has bin botherin' my stock. It might be that with the sun in our eyes, we'd just be apt to mistake a man for a coyote. A lot of your men look like coyotes. I'd shore hate to kill off any of you by accident, thataway. It's about two o'clock, by the sun. Me'n Almanac always goes huntin' about five." Long Bob turned and walked away.

A small shape slid from behind the pump-house and caught up with him. It was Little Joe.

"You shore told it scary to that big jasper," grinned Joe. "I was layin' down behind some weeds. Had him covered all the time and if he'd made a break, I'd shot a eye outa him." The boy patted his air-gun.

"Better give me that gun, Little Britches, before you git into trouble."

Bob took charge of the air-gun, smiling oddly. He had seen the boy shoot at a mark with the dangerous toy. His aim was splendid and at close range the heavy shot, almost the size of a pea, would sink a quarter inch into soft pine. He wondered just what would have been the reaction of the sheriff when a buckshot hit him in the ear or perhaps in the eye. Long Bob had been bluffing the sheriff. Runnin' a whizzer on 'im. He had no desire to become involved in a battle with these law men. But he didn't want them camped so close. A third of the posse, picked up from pool halls and saloons, were half drunk and careless about dropping lighted matches and cigarette butts. It was the fall of the year and the long grass was dry. Then again, some drunken fool might

12

take a shot at some moving object in the thick brush and willows, and cripple a horse. One of them had already shot himself accidentally. They had taken him to town with a badly torn foot.

Sim Patchen moved his camp off the Morgan-Burch land to a crossing two miles below. They stayed there almost two weeks, prowling through the rough hills in bunches, playing hide-and-seek with one another. There was plenty of whisky and poker and a few fights. Finally the sheriff got word from the county seat to bring his men in before he broke the county.

Patchen stopped at the ranch with Bull Mitchell to do some more snooping. Long Bob handed him a copy of the Helena *Record*. It gave a graphic account of a train hold-up in Wyoming. None of the train robbers had been masked. Several men had recognized them as the hard-riding, straight-shooting Wild Bunch. They also described a new member of the gang. The description fitted Wade Morgan exactly. Almanac Jones had marked that paragraph which said:

A man from Chinook, Montana, recognized the new member of the Wild Bunch as being Wade Morgan. Morgan even grinned and spoke to him. Waade Morgan recently shot to death the wealthy ranch and mine owner, Shotgun Riley. Riley made his start in the city of Butte where he owned a gambling house and saloon. It was Wade Morgan's first crime and some term it a public service rather than a crime, for Shotgun Riley's reputation was none too savory. We predict a colorful career for Wade Morgan in the calling he has been forced into choosing. A posse of a hundred men under Sim Patchen are still running around in circles through the hills hunting the elusive Wade Morgan. It must be costing the county a few dollars to keep them well fed and, from what this reporter saw on a trip there a few days ago, supplied with Dutch courage. Bull Mitchell, partner of the late Mr. Shotgun Riley, has posted a reward of five thousand dollars, dead or alive, for the quick triggered Wade. To that is now added the customary five hundred by the railroad and express companies. Whoever collects that bounty money will have earned it well, for now that Wade Morgan has turned outlaw, he will no doubt shoot first and do his questioning later. He is traveling in fast company and his case is not unlike that of the notorious Kid Curry who killed Pike Landusky a few years back. If Wade is in need of tutoring, the fast shooting, swift riding Kid is an excellent teacher.

13

Patchen, white around the lips with anger, rode away. Bob looked at Almanac Jones and grinned.

"He acted kinda mad about it, didn't he?"

Almanac Jones picked up the paper from the ground where the irate sheriff had thrown it. The old trail boss and gun fighter smoothed it out and folded it carefully. There was a hungry sort of yearning on his leathery old face and his blue eyes were bright.

"I'd give a purty tuh be ridin' with 'em, Bob. But I'm too damned stove-up. There was a time when I'd uh gone with Wade. Gone like a shot."

"It's a fool's game," said Long Bob.

"And I'm the man as knows it, Bob. But Godamighty, son, it's a game that sends a man's blood into circulation."

Long Bob smiled tolerantly.

"Don't be puttin' any fool notions into Little Britches. I don't want him tuh play the fool. When he starts growin' up, he's gonna have tuh be rode with a spade bit. No hackamore kin ever hold 'im."

The following week, Long Bob and Hattie Morgan were married by the new preacher at Chinook. Joe went along. Almanac Jones got drunk and stayed that way for a week, celebrating. Hattie nursed him back to health again and the old fellow whistled tunelessly as he puttered around the barn, little Joe trailing behind him.

Little Joe saw his first round-up that fall. He was given a string of three gentle ponies and allowed to work through until the first shipment. Then he was sent to school. There had been no word from Wade Morgan.

Chapter Three

THE FROZEN EAR

THE SCHOOL was a log building set in the scrub pines under the rimrock hills on Antelope Creek. Joe rode to school on his pony, as did most of the others. Some came in buggies or sleds when the snow got deep. About twenty-five youngsters that varied in age from seven and eight to seventeen and eighteen. The older boys worked with cattle and horses. That was their life. Tanned, husky, swaggering more than a little. Two of them packed six-shooters and rode broncs to school. They smoked and chewed and cussed and told what they'd do to the new he-schoolmarm.

The young man who had come out to teach was just out of college. He was pale looking and wore glasses and was timid of manner. The older boys ran the school and the cowed and miserable he-schoolmarm lasted only two weeks.

The next one to come was a spinster who left because the boys spit tobacco juice on the floor and told her to go to hell.

The school board sent for a big man who could handle the situation. The two Clanton boys roped him and made out as if they were going to brand him. He walked all the way to town and sent somebody back after his clothes.

All this was not such good training for a boy of Joe's age and temperament. He was allowed to ride home with the Clanton boys—they were the ones who packed guns and rode broncs and chewed. They let Joe trail with them because they knew Joe's father was the notorious Wade Morgan of the Wild Bunch. Joe tried to learn to smoke and chew and got deathly sick.

The school board, composed of cowmen, met and discussed the situation. Below the school section where stood the school, lived Doc Steele. He had quit practicing medicine some years before on account of bad health and had bought a small ranch where he and his wife and small daughter lived. He was a tall, wiry man with a fund of jokes and stories and he had a way with youngsters which made them like him.

"I'll take over that job of pounding some book learning into this wild gang of ours," he said. "I taught school once or twice and can pass the board of examiners if they won't make it too tough on me."

"Reckon you kin handle these young 'uns, Doc?" asked a grizzled cattleman.

"I'll make a try at it," smiled Doc Steele, his eyes lighting up. "I brought nearly all of 'em into the world. They know me and like me."

His lanky frame sprawled in a chair, Bill Clanton, father of the two oldest and toughest boys in school, grinned crookedly and said nothing. Bill Clanton was the only man in the community that didn't like Doc Steele. Doc had caught him red-handed, butchering a neighbor's steer and had told the big, raw-boned cattle thief that if he caught him a second time, he'd turn him over to the law. Clanton, a bushwhacker by breeding and inclination, a coward at heart, had vowed to himself that some day Doc Steele would get what was acomin' to him. Bill Clanton took pride in the swaggering toughness of Tug and Tim, his two hulking sons. He grinned at their boastings and encouraged them in their petty crimes. More than one calf that wore the Clanton iron had been "picked up" by Tug and Tim.

Perhaps Doc Steele saw that crooked grin on Bill Clanton's wide mouth, for the doctor's smile lost a little of its cheeriness.

"While I think of it," said Doc, "we need a new padlock for the saddle room at the school barn. Somebody broke in the other night and stole some things left there by the children. Halters and hackamores and tie ropes, an ax and shovel, and some other tools that belonged to the school. A petty larceny trick and whoever did it should be given a nice coat of tar and feathers. But things like that are hard to prove. I'll put on a lock that will make the burglaring a little harder.

"Getting back to the subject of teaching. Anybody object to me taking the job?"

"Hell, no!"

"Have at it, Doc!"

"And whatever yuh do, we're backin' yuh."

"Then," smiled Doc Steele, "that settles that. School opens Monday."

Monday morning was bright and clear. A Chinook wind was melting the snow from the ridges. Doc Steele and Amy, his six-year-old daughter, were there first. Doc put up his buggy horse and built a roaring fire in the big stove. The other youngsters came, excited and pleased because Doc, as they all called him, was to be their new teacher. Joe Morgan rode up with Tug and Tim Clanton. Joe came from the barn with a sort of guilty, shamed look in his eyes.

Joe had, on the way over, heard Tim and Tug boasting. They had a pint of whisky and kept drinking. They told little Joe that they were going to "make a damn bunch quitter outa Doc Steele, the skinny blue-legged sandhill crane." Joe had listened with some misgivings because he liked the genial Doc and he knew that Long Bob and Wade Morgan thought a lot of Doc.

Tug and Tim came in half an hour late. They were tipsy and flopped in their seats, their loose mouths leering. Doc paid them little notice. The other youngsters whispered in awed undertones and passed furtive notes of speculation.

Doc's indifference galled the two Clanton bullies. They began a series of half-defiant hoodlum pranks. Dipping the pig-tails of girls in inkwells, throwing spit-balls, leaving the room without permission and clumping back, their high-heeled boots making so much noise on the bare floor that recitations were momentarily halted until the big troublemakers took their seats again. Still Doc Steele ignored them and spoke no word of reprimand. The third time the two Clantons swaggered out the door, Doc Steele rose from his chair on the raised platform.

"You young folks stay in your seats until I return. In your seats does not mean getting up and running around. I'm putting you on your honor. The boy that would break his word of honor is a mighty low down sort of man."

Doc went outside. The door closed behind him. A hush fell over the classroom.

From out near the barn came queer sorts of sounds. Loud words, a yelp of pain, thudding sounds. Then a shot ripped out. Some of the girls began to cry. Little Amy Steele, sitting next to Joe, was white as chalk. Joe twisted nervously in his seat. Seconds, ticked off with startling clarity by the big wall clock, seemed hours.

They jumped when the door opened. Doc Steele stood there, wiping the wet snow from his feet. Then he entered, closing the door behind him. He walked up onto the platform. There was an ugly bruise on one cheek and his hand bled a little. His coat was ripped and his tie twisted. He smoothed his ruffled hair and with a soft chuckle, took two big six-shooters from his hip pockets and laid them down on the desk. From another pocket he took a half emptied flask of whisky and stood it boldly beside the two guns.

"Have any more of you bold, bad men got guns or hard licker on your hip?" Doc's smile was genial. The girls quit sobbing and the boys relaxed and grinned. They were all under fourteen and much smaller than the Clantons. They appreciated Doc's joke. That is, all save little Joe Morgan. He was a little white and his eyes were dark with emotion. He got on his feet and in a queer, husky little voice, he spoke.

"I got a gun out in the barn."

Doc Steele nodded gravely. An awful hush again gripped the room. Little Amy Steele trembled and her lips quivered. Tears welled to her soft brown eyes. With all her small child's heart, Amy adored Joe.

"You'd better go out to the barn, Joe, and bring in that gun."

"Yes, sir."

Joe went out. The customary swagger, borrowed from the Clantons, was gone from his stride. He ran all the way to the barn. From the home-made saddle scabbard, Joe dragged his air-gun, most highly treasured of all his possessions. He paused for a moment. From inside the saddle room where spare halters and things were locked after school, there came strange, muffled sounds. Thudding blows against the heavy door. Voices choked with anger and fright. Sounds of sobbing. Joe listened. No doubting the fact that the two Clanton toughs were bawling like six-year-olds. The door was padlocked. Joe went back into the school-house, carrying his air-gun. His jaw was set firmly and when he stepped up on the platform and handed it into Doc's hands, the boy's eyes met the man's without flinching. An older person would have caught a strange twinkle in the eyes of Doc Steele—a twinkle that was a strange mixture of mirth and pity.

"You can have your gun back some day, Joe. We've always been good partners, you and I. I don't think you had any bad motive in packing a gun to school. Suppose we shake hands and be friends for keeps. Want to shake on it, Joe?"

Joe blinked hard. He could take punishment. He had expected some sort of punishment. But something in Doc's comradeship pinched the boy's heart and he couldn't keep back the tears. He shook hands gravely with Doc. He did not know that that hand-clasp was the beginning of a staunch comradeship that was to carry them both into strange situations and dangers. The boy walked back to his seat. Amy smiled at him through a mist of tears. Joe, afraid of girls individually and collectively, ignored her little gesture and took his seat, his fists gougings the tears from his eyes. He barely heard Doc's next words.

"Since this is our first day together, I think we should celebrate," Doc was saying. "We'll put the books in the desks and have a spelling bee. Then we'll play some other games and after that I've got a surprise for you. It's too bad that Tug and Tim have to miss it all."

Tragedy became joy. Sobs turned to laughter. Doc laid an understanding hand on Joe's head and rumpled the thick curls. Joe looked up and tried to smile.

"Come on outside with me, Joe. I want some help carrying in a package or two."

The package or two proved to be a box of oranges, candy, cake and sandwiches. There was a grand snowball fight, Doc and the girls against the boys. Then they came in, were duly brushed off and fed, then dismissed and given a half holiday. The Clantons ate their cold lunches in the saddle room.

When the youngsters had all gone home, Doc Steele unlocked the door of the saddle room and stood in the doorway. In his arms he held a pile of blankets and fur robes. He tossed them inside.

"You two young hoodlums are going to spend the night in here. In the morning you'll be sent home. I'll have a talk with your father to-night."

"Pap'll kill yuh, damn yuh."

"I think not. He's the yellow-backed sire of yellow-backed whelps. He won't kill anybody except from the brush. If you feel at all lucky, you can step out and try to whip me. But if

18

you do, I'll take you both to a cleaning that will linger in your memories for many a year."

He locked them in and drove home, Amy beside him in the old top buggy that had traveled on a thousand journeys of mercy through heat and blizzard and rain and darkness. Mrs. Steele met him, an anxious look in her eyes.

"For a man of fifty, honey, and an invalid, I did rather well. I don't look for any more trouble at school."

He told her of his fight with the Clanton boys. There was an odd softness in his voice when he told her about little Joe Morgan.

"He has the makings of a brilliant gentleman, if only he don't make some fatal mistake that will send him along his father's trail. He has the keenest mind in school. Old Almanac, I think, is partly responsible for the boy's ability to read so well and spell. He's hungry for learning, too. And he has principle and courage —and the heavy burden of Morgan heritage."

Doc Steele drove over to the Clanton ranch. Bill Clanton met him with an uneasy grin.

"Tug and Tim won't be home until morning, Bill. They tried their rough tactics on me and I thrashed hell out of 'em and locked 'em up in the saddle room. They're there all night and if you make any move to release them, I'll make you sweat on the county jail rock pile."

"You locked my boys up? By God, Steele, I'll make you pay fer this. I'll get even."

"I don't doubt but you'll try, Bill. I'm sending your boys home in the morning. They'll stay home until they make up their minds that I'm running the school. Personally, I don't give a damn whether they come back or not. They're the pair that broke into the saddle room last week. They're a pair of thieving whelps and they get it naturally from you. While I'm here, fetch out the halters and other stuff they took and put it in my buggy."

"I don't know nothin' about—"

Doc leaped from his buggy, a dangerous glint in his eyes. "Get that stolen stuff, Bill Clanton, or I'll thrash hell out of you here in your own yard."

Bill Clanton slouched off. Doc followed him into the barn. Followed him back when Bill Clanton returned to the buggy, his arms piled with the stolen things.

Doc climbed back into the seat, picking up the reins. Bill Clanton, his tobacco-soiled mouth twisting, shook a bony fist at him.

"I'm a tax-payer. My young 'uns is 'titled to go to school. I'll take it up at next meetin'. Them boys uh mine is goin' to school."

"Not till they can come decently, they won't, Bill. You can't bluff me and your two overgrown sons can't run any whizzer on me. I've been here in this country too long to take water from such a tribe as yours. You're a bad neighbor, Clanton, and you'd better watch your step. I let you beg off once. So did Bob Burch. Bob caught you branding a yearling of his and you whined and slobbered out of it. I warn you now. Go slow or you may get a covering of tar and feathers and a ride on a rail. You come from down in Missouri so I reckon you know what a rail ride means. So-long, Clanton. Mind you stay clear away from that school section to-night."

Doc clucked to his fat old horse and drove off. He knew that he had made an enemy and a bad one. But he whistled cheerily all the way home as the fat bay gelding paced along the sloppy road that was beginning to freeze.

Over at the Morgan-Burch ranch, little Joe gave his audience of three a graphic description of what had happened. With a grave little face he told of surrendering his air-gun to Doc. Nobody laughed.

"Doc was right, Little Britches," said Long Bob. "The Clantons are a ornery lot. You stay clear of Tug and Tim Clanton, or they'll git you into trouble. Doc Steele is a fine man. If folks paid Doc what's comin' to him, he'd be a millionaire. He like to kill hisse'f drivin' all over the country tendin' sick folks. He come thirty miles in a blizzard once to set the busted leg of a forty dollar cowhand and wouldn't take a dime. The night you was born, Joe, Doc Steele set up all night and didn't want tuh take any money for the work he done savin' yore mother's life. He's loaned money he never got back. He's a man, Little Britches. The Clantons are skunks."

"And Mollie Steele is the kindest woman in the world," announced Hattie stoutly. Both men knew what she meant. Some of the town women had treated Hattie shabbily when they learned that she was living with Wade Morgan without the formality of a marriage ceremony. Mollie Steele had told those women, in no uncertain terms, her views on the subject. She had defended Hattie with a fervor that was rarely found among women in defense of their kind.

Little Joe listened in silence while the two men and the woman talked of Doc Steele and his missus. They were still on the subject when the boy fell asleep on the floor alongside the stove, a hound pup on either side of him.

That was the winter that little Joe saved Amy Steele from freezing to death in a blizzard. In doing so, one of his ears was so badly frozen that it was necessary to amputate part of it. But he had saved the life of Amy. It marked a definite spot along Joe's forward trail, because it gave him the everlasting gratitude of Doc Steele. That meant the influence in Joe's life of a man who talked of books rather than guns. It was an influence that was to be felt strongly in the difficult years that were coming.

The Clanton boys did not return to school. They stayed home with their old man and waited for the right chance to even up with Doc Steele. At the Clanton ranch, during the long winter evenings, many plans were discussed and abandoned as being too risky. Bill Clanton's wife took part in these conferences. She was a shrill-tongued, angular, slatternly female with buck teeth. She dipped snuff and went bare-footed in summer. When the snow came, she wore a pair of Bill's shoes and one of his coats when she went to town. Her hands were the hands of a man and she could fork hay with Bill or her boys, shock for shock, swear like a mule skinner, and drink her share of the moonshine whisky they made and sold secretly. Smarter than her men folks, she voted down their various plans.

"Wait," she told them. "The time's a-comin'. Raise a hand now and we'll be run outa here like we bin run outa other places. Wait." And she showed her yellow teeth in a hideous grin.

"A man gits tired a-waitin'," complained Bill.

"Git tired, damn yore gizzard. You'll wait. Then I'll show yuh how tuh git even. Make out tuh be friends with the damn ——s around here. So they won't suspect. Then there'll come a day when I'll show yuh a trick worth ten that'd come from yore wooden head."

So the Clanton tribe waited. Reared in a feud-ridden country, they knew how to wait. Bill and the boys confined their hate to petty stealing and whisky peddling. A few stolen calves, an occasional beef. In early spring a sheepherder over on the forks of Squaw Creek got drunk on a jug of moonshine and froze to death in a snowstorm. The wolves got into his scattered band of ewes. They ripped and slashed their way through the panicky sheep, crippling and killing. The rest of the sheep piled up against a cut bank and smothered one another in their terror. The owner of the sheep was a Dane who had, five years ago, fired Bill Clanton who was working with a lambing crew. . . . So Bill had waited. . . . And there had been no proof that he had sold the jug of whisky to the herder.

A few weeks in jail, then he was back. That was Bill Clanton's way.

That March, a train was held up somewhere in Kansas. One night in June a stranger rode into the Morgan-Burch ranch and asked for Long Bob. He handed Bob a letter and a bulging muslin sack. Then he rode away.

The note was from Wade Morgan. Briefly worded, it wished Hattie and Bob much happiness. It spoke rather vaguely of his life:

These boys are sure fine boys. Just like home folks. Butch is a comical cuss sometimes but he's game as hell. So is the Kid and the others. We have some good times and some tough ones. We buried a boy last week that got shot up bad. He died cussin the man that got him but felt better when he found out I had rode back and gutshot the feller. . . . From where I am sittin on this pinnacle I kin see the big butte near the ranch with my glasses. Wisht I could pay you all a visit but I got a 30-30 slug in one leg a while back and it ain't healed so good yet. Best regards to you all. Am sending you a weddin present. Spend it and think of me. There's plenty more where this come from. *Burn this letter.*

There were five thousand dollars in the muslin sack. Long Bob put the money in an empty tobacco can and hid it under the floor of the barn. He told Hattie and Almanac Jones where he had put it.

"It might come in handy some day, Hattie. Somehow I don't feel like usin' it. We got all we need to live on. It might bring us bad luck. But if Wade ever gets caught and has tuh stand trial, it'll come in handy."

"Bob's right," said old Almanac Jones. "Plumb right."

School was out now and Bob took little Joe along with him to the calf round-up. They worked around with the Long-X wagon and then with a pool outfit over on Milk River. Everybody liked Long Bob and when they worked in close to his place, they gave Bob more than his share of mavericks. Joe was teased and spoiled. He was beginning already to show signs of cow-savvy. He knew brands, he remembered the range they crossed. He did anything he was told without question or complaint. From boss to cook, Joe was well liked.

The first day of July found Long Bob and Joe with their string of horses, their pack-horse, and a small bunch of cows and calves, back on their home range. They turned their cows and calves loose on good feed and water, then rode on to the ranch—an unshaven, overalled, happy Bob, a tanned, rather dirty, eager-eyed Joe, bursting with the many tales he would tell his mother and Almanac.

Hattie met them at the barn. Bob read the worried look in her eyes. He knew that something was wrong.

"What is it, Hattie?" he asked, holding her in his arms while she tried to hug both Bob and Joe at once.

"Sim Patchen was here, Bob. He took Almanac to jail."

"What's Almanac been up to?"

"Nothing, Bob. But last week we needed fresh beef for the hay crew. Almanac butchered one of our two-year-olds and hung the hide on the corral. The next morning a little after daylight, Bull Mitchell and Sim Patchen rode up. Said they wanted to see the hide of that beef Almanac had butchered. He took them out to the corral. There was a hide there, a fresh hide, but it wasn't the one Almanac had hung there. It had Bull Mitchells iron on it. So they took Almanac to jail. The old fellow made me promise not to send you word. Said he'd stay in jail till you got home. He didn't want you to quit in the middle of the calf work."

"Got any idea who might have switched them hides?" asked Bob. "Somebody here at the ranch must have known when Almanac butchered. They musta planted somebody here."

"The hay crew are all breeds—Pete La Frombois and his boys and the La Valleys. They wouldn't do a dirty trick like that. But the evening Almanac butchered, the Clanton boys stopped for supper."

Bob threw his saddle on a fresh horse and got his Winchester from the gun rack. Without shaving or stopping to change clothes, he rode off. Hattie and Joe watched him ride away. He turned in his saddle and waved his hat. They waved back. Then he topped the ridge and was gone from sight. Hattie and little Joe were alone.

"I'll take care of you," said little Joe. She bent and knelt there, her arms around her small son, her eyes misty.

Chapter Four

NIGHT RIDERS

LONG BOB rode straight to the Clanton ranch and called Bill Clanton outside. He shoved the barrel of a six-shooter into the lanky Missourian's belly and thumbed back the hammer.

"Dig up that hide of mine, Clanton, or by God, I'll kill you where yuh stand."

Bill Clanton opened his mouth to say something. When his eyes met Long Bob's eyes, his jaw hung open. Because he knew that Long Bob meant exactly what he said.

"Don't shoot, Burch! I'll git yore hide."

Long Bob followed him up into the haymow. The hide, cut in half and rolled with the hair side out, was buried under the hay.

"Now saddle up and come on to town, Clanton. Where's them boys of yourn?"

"In town, Burch, drunk. They done it. I told 'em not to. But Bull Mitchell paid 'em good."

Together, the hide on the back of Bob's saddle, they rode into town. It was getting dusk as they rode up the one dusty street and halted at a log cabin that bore the sign 'Justice of the Peace." The Justice was a one-legged old shyster with a smattering of law in a whisky-soaked brain. He sat there, his peg leg on a liquor-spotted desk, talking to Sim Patchen who lounged in an arm-hair of the variety popular in bar-rooms. He bore the odd name of Jim Love. Better know as Peg Leg.

Long Bob prodded Bill Clanton in the back with his six-shooter. Clanton, green with fear, stumbled into the littered office, carrying the green hide in his arms.

"Don't go for that gun of yourn, Patchen," said Bob quietly, "or I'll gut-shoot yuh. That goes for you, Peg Leg. Now, you two skunks will take a look at the brand on this hide and tell me what it is. Spread out the hide on the floor, Clanton."

"Looky here, Burch," snarled Patchen, "you can't do this!"

"Spread out the hide, Clanton. Shut up, Patchen. You, you one-legged snake, slide out from behind that desk. You ain't got the guts to pick up the gun that's there. Step out."

Bob made them read the brand aloud. It was the Morgan-Burch iron, Rafter Y.

"That's the hide that goes with the beef Almanac Jones butchered. Peg Leg, skin out of here and go up to the jail. Unlock Almanac Jones and fetch him here. If you stop to talk to anybody or if you and Almanac ain't here in five minutes, I'll give Sim Patchen the damnedest gun whippin' a human ever got in his life."

Peg Leg looked at the sheriff. "Drag it," snapped Patchen. "The damn fool is loco enough to do it."

"And take Bill Clanton along with you, Peg Leg," said Long Bob. "Lock him up and keep him there. Because when this gets out, some of the white folks around here might make it hot fer him. Git the idea, Clanton?"

When Peg Leg and the thoroughly frightened Bill Clanton had gone, Long Bob grinned mirthlessly at Sim Patchen.

"I got the goods on Bull Mitchell this time. Bill Clanton and his coyote sons will spill their guts when they come up for trial. Know what that means for you, Patchen? You'll be back tendin' bar and dealin' crooked cards, and it'll be in a climate that'll fit yore clothes. Once Bull Mitchell quits this range, you'll be like a mammyless calf at a roundup."

"You'll play hell makin' Bull Mitchell quit this range, Burch. He's got plenty money and plenty friends and while you may win this hand, the game ain't over. We'll hang your hide on the fence some day."

"Like you hung Wade Morgan's" grinned Long Bob. "Yo're more harmless than a gut-eatin' reservation squaw, Patchen. If you was half a man you wouldn't be lettin' me git away with this."

"You haven't got away with it yet. Gimme an even break and by God, I'll—"

"All right. If that's what yore cravin'." Long Bob shoved his .45 back in its holster and raised both hands. His slitted eyes were holding those of the sheriff whose pudgy hand was on his gun.

"Well, Patchen, here's yore even break. Better than even. Fill yore hand, you pot-bellied gopher."

But Sim Patchen was like a man paralyzed. His face was mottled, his restless eyes congested, but his hand slid away from his gun. Long Bob grinned his contempt.

Peg Leg came in with Almanac Jones. The old fellow was gaunt and starved-looking but he managed a grin when he saw Bob.

"I knowed you'd be comin', Bob. But I thought these snakes 'ud starve me afore you made it. They fed me the leavin's from the Chink's restaurant. Them was Bull Mitchell's orders."

"Give Almanac his gun, Peg Leg."

When the snarling old Justice of the Peace had done this, and Almanac was fondling his old white-handled six-shooter, Bob gave his next order.

"Let's have a look at that jail, Patchen. Rattle yore hocks. You, too, Peg Leg."

Five minutes later Almanac and Long Bob strolled down from the jail together.

"When we git Bull Mitchell and the Clanton kids in there, we'll have a full house," grinned Bob.

They found the two Clantons in Shotgun Riley's saloon. They were standing at the bar, drinking and talking loudly to an audience composed mostly of bar-room bums and miners off shift. Nobody noticed Long Bob's entrance. He came up behind the two Clantons, reached out with both hands, and cracked their heads together—once, twice, and a third time. Then he propelled them across the floor and outside. Almanac stood beside the door, his gun in his hand, grinning widely.

Ten minutes later they were back. Bob walked up to the bar. "Where's Bull Mitchell?"

"He pulled out this mornin', Burch. Honest to God. Went down to the ranch."

"Then slide out a quart of your best whisky and charge it to profit and loss."

"Take it and welcome, Burch. The way you give them two mouthy Clantons the bum's ruch, was worth two quarts. Only that Bull gimme orders to pass 'em all they could drink, I'd have done the same. Here's two quarts. Drink hearty. I'm quitting this damn job, anyhow. That's the straight goods about Bull headin' for the ranch."

The barn man confirmed the bartender's statement. Long Bob and Almanac rode out of town. Almanac threw the jail keys into the creek as they crossed. Bob pulled the cork on a bottle of Bull Mitchell's private stock. Almanac took a long, gurgling drink and passed back the bottle, a wide grin lighting his seamed face.

"Whichaway now, Bob?"

"Bull Mitchell's ranch," said Long Bob grimly. "This boil has come to a head and Bull Mitchell is the head. I'm gonna bust that head."

"Don't go playin' the fool, son," cautioned the older man. "Mind now, yuh got Hattie and the boy tuh think about."

"There won't be any killin'," promised Long Bob.

A man on horseback was coming toward them. Out of the darkness they could hear the click of shod hoofs on the rocky road. Bob and Almanac rode apart so that the rider must pass between them. Their guns were ready—an unnecessary precaution, however, for the rider was Doc Steele. The doctor's voice betrayed his relief at seeing them.

"I heard you were in jail, Almanac, and rode over to the ranch. Hattie told me that Bob had come to town so I came on up to see how things were going. You haven't done anything rash, have you, Bob?"

"Nothin' they kin hang me for, Doc." He told briefly about

locking Peg Leg, Sim Patchen, and the three Clantons in the stout log jail.

"Where are you going now, boys?" asked Doc Steele pointedly.

"No use tryin' tuh lie about it, Doc. I'm headed fer Bull Mitchell's ranch. I aim to whup him until he can't stand. There won't be no gun play."

"Mind if I go along, Bob?"

"If you feel thataway, Doc. Yuh might come in handy, pullin' Bull offen me. I ain't right positive I'm man enough tuh clean him."

"Out of the mouths of babes, loco folks, and cowhands," voiced Almanac sagely, feeling his liquor, "cometh words of wisdom. Bull's no slouch with his dukes."

The three rode on. Almanac Jones waxed mellow and loquacious. Doc Steele always enjoyed the old gun-man when he was in was in his cups. Almanac would gather bits of quotations, scripture, poetry and half-remembered song and piece the bits into an amazing whole that tickled the genial doctor.

"As this here Sodom says to Gommorey, them as sows wild oats shall reap nothin' but a crop uh rollin' stones and a gentle ox in the pasture is worth ten wild 'uns in the bush. And while Bull Shakespeare and Danny Webster and Ben Franklin always claimed that the Golden Rule beat the rules of the Marquis of Queensberries, I'm here to state, gents and gentle Annies, that if that first blow is a hard 'un, him as wields the same has the fight wropped around his gun barrel."

Almanac pulled the back of a horny hand across his bearded lips and reached for the bottle.

"The second quart is always the sweetest. May the Northern lights never dim and the howlin' wolves never cease till Bull Mitchell's planted deep where the skunks kin make a trail acrost his unmarked grave. Here's howdy."

Half an hour passed. An hour. Almanac sang, in a mournful key, "Sam Bass" and "Rock of Ages," using one tune for both songs. Doc called him an economist on tunes. Almanac knew the words, or some of the words, to innumerable songs. The tune was always the same.

They came to the gate that led to the Mitchell place. The ranch was some three miles below the gate which opened into a huge pasture.

The moon had come up and now, coming haltingly up the road, plainly revealed in the pale light, was a horse with an empty saddle. The horse traveled crab-wise, head held to one side to avoid stepping on the trailing reins. The horse was a big buckskin. Bull Mitchell's town horse.

Bob leaned over and picked up the buckskin's dragging bridle reins. He swung to the ground and straightened the saddle that had partly turned.

"Get off, Doc," he said in a flat tone, "and see what you make of this."

Doc dismounted. He struck a match and held it in his cupped hands. He and Long Bob examined the dark, sticky stains on the saddle and the mane of the horse.

"It's blood all right, Bob. And a lot of it. Fresh, too. Looks like something has happened to Mitchell."

"Let us hope," said Almanac softly, "that it's plenty bad. I'd be proud tuh shove his carcass in to a coyote hole and tromp dirt in his face."

"I'm glad," said Doc, swinging back into his saddle, "that I came along. Otherwise, Bob, you'd be accused of this killing, providing Bull Mitchell is dead."

"True, brother Steele, true," crooned Almanac. "Now let's ease along yonder trail and view the demised remains of our esteemed and sheep-stealin' citizen, the Honorable Bullock Mitchell.

> Oh, he fought men fer marbles,
> He fought men fer fun.
> But he's jerked his last trigger,
> He's fanned his last gun."

They found Bull Mitchell about a mile and a half down the road. Lighting matches, Almanac kept humming mournfully. Doc Steele's quick hands probing in under the blue flannel shirt that was soggy with blood. Bull Mitchell moaned through clenched teeth and his eyes opened. Bloodshot eyes that flickered with fear when they recognized Long Bob Burch.

"Damn lucky for you, Mitchell," Doc Steele was saying, "that it was a steel jacket bullet and it went a couple of inches high. You've lost a lot of blood but you'll be all right in a few weeks unless there's infection."

"Hell," grunted Almanac Jones disgustedly and blew out the match he was holding.

"Who shot yuh?" asked Long Bob.

"None of your God-damned business, Burch. Gimme a drink."

"Go to hell," snapped Almanac Jones. "I'd ruther smash the bottle."

"Is there any one at your place, Mitchell," asked Doc Steele, "that can look after you?"

"Yes. Pack me there. Then get to hell off my land."

"If you wait till I lend a hand packin' yuh," growled Almanac, "yuh'll die of old age. Come on home, Bob."

But Bob helped Doc put Bull Mitchell on his horse and hold him in the saddle. Much to Almanac's disgust, Bob gave Bull a stiff drink from the bottle.

"Hope it infects yuh, Mitchell," the old fellow grunted.

They got Bull Mitchell to his ranch and the man and woman who stayed there got a bed ready. Bob stayed to help the doctor but Almanac Jones rode on home, swearing like a pirate and complaining bitterly that fate let men like Bull Mitchell live.

The road that led from the Bull Mitchell place to the Morgan-Burch pace cut across a corner of the Mitchell pasture. There were two gates to open. Drunk as he was, Almanac Jones noticed the blood smears on the gate sticks. Both gates, wire gates they were, lay on the ground as if whoever opened them had done so without leaving the saddle. It was when Almanac got off to close the gates, thereby following the unwritten law of the cow country that a man never leaves open the gate of friend or enemy, that he discovered the blood.

As he rode homeward, Almanac puzzled it out. Bull Mitchell had been shot somewhere in the vicinity of the Morgan-Burch place. Shocked into sudden fear, Almanac stowed away his bottle and spurred his horse to a long lope that ate up the miles. He came off the ridge and down into the home ranch on a run. Before his horse had slid to a halt, Almanac was on the ground and at the door of the house. He gave a gasping grunt of relief when he saw Hattie and little Joe in the front room.

Hattie Morgan was pale and visibly upset. Little Joe, white-lipped but trying to hide the fear in his heart, stood in front of her. In his small hands was the Winchester carbine that had belonged to Hattie's father. When Joe recognized Almanac, he laid the heavy gun on the table and tried to smile.

Where's Bob?" cried Hattie.

"Safe, honey. What's gone wrong here? Was Bull Mitchell here?"

"Yes," Her voice quivered a little.

"He came here, Almanac, right after Doc Steele left. I was in the kitchen and he came in there without knocking. He was drunk, Almanac. He—he grabbed me and I broke away. Joe was in here. I ran in here. I didn't see Joe. Not until he shot at Mitchell. . . . Then I saw him, Almanac, standing behind the sofa, pointing the smoking gun at Mitchell. He told Mitchell that if he took another step, he'd kill him. He meant it. His little voice was terrible. Mitchell was afraid to come any further. Joe told him to go or he'd kill him. Mitchell went."

She collapsed weakly on the couch. Joe's color had come back into his cheeks but he was trembling. Almanac took the carbine and put it back in the rack.

"We found Mitchell," Almanac said. "I reckon he'll make a live of it. That is, unless Bob finds out what happened here. Then Bob'll kill him. And if Bob does that, he'll be sent to the pen, sure as hell. So we got to keep quiet. Joe, you acted mighty brave this evenin'. Braver than most men. But we'll have to keep this a secret between us. Promise?"

"You bet," nodded Joe.

"You know what I mean, Hattie?"

"Of course. Bob mustn't ever know."

"I'll have a pow-wow with Mitchell. He ain't told yet, and he won't, bet on that, when I talk turkey to him. I reckon that Bob and Doc will leave there by the upper gate because they'll be together and they'll go past Doc's place. I heard Doc tell Bob that he wanted to stop there on the way home. Somethin' about sendin' Joe away to a good school. Bob said to tell you he might stay there all night and not to worry about him. So they won't see the blood on the gate sticks. And we'll just keep this all a secret. Now, Joe, you dog-goned old wart-hog, let's rustle ol' Almanac some grub and coffee as yore mother jest sets there and takes it easy."

"Sit, nothing." Hattie was recovering from her shock and fright. "I'm the cook in this house. Almanac, you look as ga'nt as a dogie steer after a hard winter."

"Which," grinned the old trail boss, "exactly describes the way my stomach feels. I'm as ga'nt as a rawhide rope. I'll put up my hoss."

Almanac tended to his horse and drained his bottle. He then took the unopened bottle, mate to the dead one, and carefully hid it in a manger, much after the manner of a dog burying a bone. Now and then he chuckled or swore softly. He was thinking of little Joe, son of Wade Morgan, the killer.

"The danged li'l' ol' son of a gun. Takin' a pop at Bull Mitchell, and Bull a gun fighter and a good 'un. The danged li'l' ol' wart-hog."

Then he sobered, a troubled look creeping into his eyes. He was remembering Wade Morgan.

So it happened that the next morning, when Doc Steele and Long Bob told Hattie and Almanac of a plan to send little Joe away next fall to a military school, Almanac was strongly in favor of the idea.

"Joe is too brilliant a lad," said Doc, "to be held back in a country school. He needs proper instruction and he needs outside contacts. He'll live in a barracks with several hundred other boys. He'll learn discipline and countless other things that will fit him for life. I went there for nine years and I look back upon those years as formative. Also, I like to remember them as being the happiest years of my youth. Once Joe gets acquainted, he'll like it. He can come home Christmas and for his summer vacation."

"I'm leavin' it up to you, Hattie," said Long Bob. "You and Almanac."

"It'll be the makin' of him," Almanac put in quickly. "This here ain't the best country in the world fer a growin' boy." His keen eyes found Hattie's and she nodded.

"I think, Bob," she agreed, "that it would be a great thing for Joe to get away from here and meet other boys."

"I'll fix up his credits and get him registered," smiled Doc Steele. "And when I go east next month, I'll take Joe back with me. You'll never regret this step. Never. I'm thinking of Joe as if he were my own boy."

So it came about that Joe Morgan, son of Wade Morgan, outlaw, went east to the best military academy in the United States.

Almanac had a talk with Bull Mitchell and came back home, very drunk but plainly happy. Bull was more than ready to keep his mouth shut.

"Because," Almanac explained quietly, "I'll kill you, personal, Bull, if yuh don't. And if Wade Morgan was ever to hear about what you done, he'd ride up here with his friends and what they'd do to you and yore layout here would be a-plenty. Git the idee?"

As for the Clantons, no charge was lodged against them. They came home, sober, somewhat uneasy in their minds, cowardice dampening their loudly voiced bravado.

One night, a week or so later, a group of night riders visited the Clanton ranch. These men were masked and armed. One of them carried three ropes hung in the crook of his arm. Bill Clanton, his blasphemous wife, and his two stalwart sons were called outside.

There was some light wrom a waning moon. It revealed their faces, white and drawn with abject fright. A noose went around each of their necks. The woman cursed them all with rasping, half-sane fervor. A fourth noose came into view. It went around her scrawny neck and her cursing became more subdued and then ceased. These silent men with black hoods masking their faces meant business.

"Don't!" screamed the woman. "My God, don't! Have mercy!

We'll do anything yuh want of us! Don't kill us! God, oh, God!"

The ropes slacked a little. The spokesman of the silent, hooded riders spoke to the Clanton's in dry, brittle words. When he ceased talking, their frightened tongues croaked out promises. At a curt order from the spokesman. The ropes were loosened.

"Break yore promises and we'll come back," he told the Clantons. "And if we come again, the four of you will stretch rope." They rode away into the night as swiftly as they had come.

Chapter Five

AN OUTLAW OPERATION

SIX YEARS had come and gone past. It was June and a full moon rode the sky. There came a cautious knock at Doc Steele's door. Doc, preparing for bed, answered the summons. Bob Burch stood there in the moonlight.

"Git into yore clothes, Doc, and fetch yore tool bag. There's a man at my place that's bin shot."

"Be with you in a jiffy, Bob. Come in."

"No, I'll saddle up yore horse."

They rode away together in the night. But they did not ride in the direct of Bob's ranch. Instead they took a seldom used trail that led past the Clanton place and down into the bad-lands— five hours of hard riding.

Long Bob pulled up his horse.

"You ain't asked ary question, Doc, and I'm obliged. It's Wade Morgan. If yuh don't mind. I'll blindfold yuh. What a man don't know, never hurts him. Just as well yuh don't know where yo're a-goin'. Then it'll save yuh lyin', mebby."

Long Bob tied a heavy black silk neckscarf across Doc's eyes. He led the doctor's horse the rest of the way. Half an hour later they halted at a long cabin hidden in a box cañon.

Some men sat around a campfire outside. Others slept in tarp-covered beds spread on the ground. Horses grazed at the end of picket ropes. The firelight flickered across blued steel gun barrels that lay on the ground within reach. A tow-headed, square-jawed man stood in the doorway of the cabin. The sleeves of his flannel shirt were rolled back and there was blood on his arms. He greeted Doc Steele with a wide grin of welcome.

"This is Doc Steele, Butch." Long Bob led the way inside the cabin.

The man called Butch wiped his hands on his overalls and rolled a cigarette.

Two lanterns lighted the cabin. Wade Morgan lay on his back on a bunk near the stove. Another man was heating some water and was washing some bloody bandages made from strips of flour sacks. He smiled thinly and nodded. A pleasant looking man, thought Doc, though the stubble of beard on his face marred the clean lines of his features.

"Howdy, Doc, you darned old sheepherder. I knowed you'd come." The voice, weak and strained, still held the reckless note that belonged to the Wade Morgan of six years ago. But Wade's face had changed—gaunt, unshaven, his eyes bloodshot and sunken with suffering. His thick, wavy hair was filled with gray. He lay on a soiled tarp, naked save for an undershirt, his left thigh wrapped in blood-stained bandages. He was propped up with blankets and a cold cigarette hung in his tightly drawn lips. There was a half emptied bottle of whisky on a bench beside the bunk. The hand he held out was white and bony. The face above the beard was sallow, save for a stain on the cheekbones. He had a tell-tale cough. Tuberculosis. His eyes met Doc's and he grinned crookedly.

"Yep. Got the bug in my lungs, Doc. Three years in the pen at Yuma did it—in under another name—I drawed five years for stealin' a damned two-bit horse that couldn't outrun a posse. They put me on a road gang and I killed a guard and got away. The boys helped me. The guard got me in the laig before I could git his cannon. It's a long ways here to Montana from Arizona when yuh got a hole in yore laig." He took a big drink of whisky. The spots on his cheekbones seemed to deepen. Doc Steele was carefully cutting away the bandages on the swollen, discolored leg. There was a grim look in the doctor's eyes.

"Don't tell me I'm gonna lose that laig, Doc." But the doctor gave him no reply. Wade looked over at the man near the stove.

"A man needs two good laigs tuh foller this gang, eh Kid?"

The man at the stove showed a set of white teeth. "Serves you right, Wade, for stealin' a horse that had three gaits. Walk, stumble, and fall down. You won't lose no laigs." It was Harvey Logan, alias Kid Curry, who spoke—the notorious Kid, quickest triggered outlaw of them all. A killer whose embittered heart knew no fear of anything that walked the earth. A loyal friend, the Kid, and an unforgiving enemy whose swift gun was wont to square his debts of hate. Dogs and horses understood him. Men who knew him would die for him. Law officers respected his fighting ability. His enemies slept uneasily of a night and kept their shades pulled low. His popularity among cowpunchers was equal to that of the genial, fun-loving, tow-headed Butch Cassidy, acknowledged leader of the Wild Bunch.

The Kid, Butch, and Long Bob now helped Doc Steele. Wade was made to lie down. The sweet, sickly odor of ether filled the little cabin. Wade lay, breathing steadily, his eyes closed. Doc's swift white hand worked smoothly with glittering, razor-edged instruments. Blood flowed in crimson blots. Cow-land surgery. Doc probed for the leaden slug and found it.

"God's will and Wade Morgan's toughness. . . . Wonder he didn't die days ago. . . . Keep the water boiling, Kid. That's the stuff, Bob, that roll of sponges." Co-land surgery. A surgeon who knew his men and his art. At last the leg was wrapped in white bandages. Many a city surgeon would have shuddered at the crudity of the operation. But those same city-bred, hospital trained men would have been unable to do as well under like conditions. Doc Steele had years of country practice behind him. He was used to coping with the crudity of conditions.

"No more whisky. He can't be moved. And he'll require careful attention. Proper diet and attention. Bob can bring me again tomorrow night. I'll leave some of these capsules. When the pain is too tough, give him one of these. He's in a weakened condition and if it was an ordinary man, I'd say his chances were worse than bad. If that infection gets much worse, the leg will have to come off at the hip."

Doc reached in under the pillow and pulled out Wade Morgan's .45. He handed it to Butch. But Butch shook his head and replaced the gun, a queer smile on his mouth.

"I'd feel like Wade'd feel if that laig has got to come off, Doc." He looked at the Kid, who nodded grimly.

"Butch is right. One laig's no good to a man in this game. They'd ketch him again. You kin see what that hell-hole at Yuma done to him."

Doc Steele understood. The gun stayed under Wade's pillow. Doc was blindfolded and taken away. It was sun-up when they rode past the Clanton place. Bill Clanton's wife and one of the boys stood near the barn and watched them ride past.

Bob left Doc at his ranch and rode home. Hattie and Joe were at the barn waiting for him. Joe was a grown man in stature now—tall, well-muscled, straight-backed from his military training. A soft-spoken, quiet-mannered young chap with a splendid record at school in athletics and in all branches of study save mathemathics. He had his arm across the shoulders of his mother. Both of them had seen the messenger who had brought word of Wade Morgan's injury. Now they waited for Bob to speak.

Time had healed the hurt of Wade's leaving. Long Bob had

more than taken Wade's place in Hattie's heart. But she still retained a certain sort of love for the outlaw. Bob understood.

As for Joe Morgan, his father was but a dim memory. He worshipped Bob Burch and always thought of him as a boy thinks of his own father. Yet there was an odd sort of love that tied him to Wade Morgan. It was, of course, a blood tie. Joe was the living replica of the Wade Morgan who had lived here at the ranch and followed the honest life of cowboy and rancher. His walk, his quick way of moving, his method of handling a horse were Wade's ways. Only in his speech and his manner toward men and women, was the son different from the father. Slow to anger, quicker to forgive, more self-contained and tolerant than Wade. Perhaps it was his training under military discipline. Or it might have been the gentler influence of his mother's blood. He was so much like his father, yet so different at times. Almanac, who studied the growing boy, was torn between worry and relief. He once told Doc Steele that it was pretty much up to God how the boy would turn out.

Long Bob met the eager question in the eyes of mother and son.

"Wade's got a fightin' chance. He's bin in the pen. Three years. That's why we never heard. He was scared to even let his gang know fer fear the prison authorities would find out who he was and hang him. He looks purty bad. It's his lungs. Prison plague. Yuma's worse than hell. Even Doc can't tell yet about the laig. Somebody's got to stay there and look after him fer a few weeks."

A harrassed look crept into Long Bob's eyes. He knew that the Wild Bunch would be moving on—drifting on down the outlaw trail. Like a pack of wolves followed by hunters. It was only a question of days until someone would blunder onto their hidden cabin, or see them hiding around. A posse would be down there. That meant death or capture for Wade Morgan. Wade, who was a crippled wolf unable to trail with the pack.

"Couldn't I go down there?" questioned Hattie.

"Wade wouldn't let yuh, honey, even if I was fool enough to let yuh go. No, it's a man's job."

"Or a boy's," put in Joe Morgan quietly. "It's my job, Bob. I'll pull out this evenin'."

Almanac Jones, who had been cleaning out a stall, had come up and stood there, leaning on his manure fork. He said nothing. Just stood there, his keen eyes reading their faces, his white-whiskered jaws working on a large cud of natural leaf plug. He saw the eager, almost reckless light that danced in Joe's eyes—a light that made them Wade's eyes. He saw Long Bob hold back his reply, torn between loyalty to Wade Morgan and his duty to Joe Morgan's future. Old Almanac breathed a deep sigh of relief as Long Bob shook his head.

"It ain't a job for a kid like you, Joe. Wade's an outlaw. Whoever he'ps him is breakin' the law. If a sheriff er two should ride down there, Wade'll fight till they kill 'im. You'd be into it, into it like a bogged steer. No, Joe, it ain't yore job."

Joe's jaw jutted stubbornly, though he still smiled. "Wade Morgan is my father, Bob. I'll pull-out this evenin'."

Almanac Jones spat largely and went back into the barn. He knew that Joe was going, with Bob's permission or without it.

"All right, Joe." Long Bob managed a grin. "But if anything turns up, you high-tail it outa there. Remember, son, you owe that much to yore mother."

Joe grinned back. It was a boy's grin.

"I won't forget her, Bob. Nor I won't forget you and Doc and Almanac. I knew what you're all worrying about. Sometimes it worries me some, too. But I don't reckon I'll ever follow Wade Morgan's trail."

He gripped his mother's shoulder and looked down into her eyes when she smiled up at him. Then he let go and swung off toward the house, humming softly, a straight-backed, handsome-looking figure of confident youth.

He went down into the bad-lands that night with Doc Steele and Long Bob. Without a blindfold, he rode into the hidden camp of the outlaws. Save for Kid Curry and the injured Wade, the camp was deserted.

"Sighted a couple of riders foxing around," explained the Kid. "So the boys drug it fer a new camp. If I'm needed here, I'll stay."

"We'll make out, Kid," said Long Bob. "How's Wade?"

"He just woke up. Kinda feverish and outa his head a little. I had tuh tie him down." He handed Bob Wade's gun. "He damn near killed me. Thought I was Shotgun Riley."

Joe Morgan followed Doc Steele inside. The boy stared hard at the gaunt, bearded, hollow-eyed man tied to the bunk. There was little about that terrible face to remind him of the father he remembered. Wade was straining doggedly at the ropes that held him fast. His lips bared away from his gritting teeth and only madness showed in his red-shot eyes.

"Damn you, Shotgun!" he rasped, staring at Doc Steele. "I'll git loose directly and I'll kill you like I'd kill any other snake." He began coughing. Pity—pity and something else akin to horror—filled Joe Morgan. Then he passed Doc and went over to the bunk. He put a hand on Wade's twiching shoulder.

"Don't you know me, Dad? It's Joe."

"Who?" Wade's mouth quit twisting. "Who?"

"Joe. Joe Morgan. Your kid."

"Little Joe?" Sanity was coming back into Wade's eyes. It was like the feeble flicker of a match in a damp cavern. It went out as quickly and he cursed Joe horribly. He called Joe a stool pigeon and a prison rat and a double-crossing warden's pet and told him he'd cut his guts out with a dull knife. Then he began laughing. Doc Steele bared Wade's forearm and jabbed in the hypodermic needle. After a while Wade's cursing stopped and Doc dressed the wounded leg.

"I'll stick," repeated the Kid, "if yuh think—"

"I'll manage," said Joe. The two were alone outside where the Kid was shoving .30-.40 shells into a cartridge belt. The outlaw looked hard at the boy.

"You look a lot like Wade usta look, button. I bet you got his sand, too. Wade's all white man."

Joe flushed a little under the famous outlaw's praise. The Kid shoved out his hand.

"So long, button. Take care uh Wade. One of us'll drop over now and then. If anybody comes nosin' around, tell 'em nothin', and damn little of that. So long." He swung into his saddle and rode away at a trot. Joe's eyes followed the outlaw out of sight. Then he went back inside the cabin to join Long Bob and Doc.

Doc Steele gave Joe directions regarding Wade's care. They had brought along a pack-horse laden with supplies. Joe displayed more than the layman's knowledge of first aid, explaining that it was a part of the school training. Some time later, Long Bob and Doc rode away, leaving the boy and his father who slept heavily, motionless as a corpse save for his breathing.

Joe sat near the bunk, studying the face of his father. He knew from the conversation between Doc, Long Bob, and the Kid, that Wade Morgan was in bad shape. The leg was badly swollen and discolored. It might mean amputation. Bob had laid Wade's gun on a shelf above the bunk.

"Don't let him get to it, Joe."

Joe understood. Wade Morgan with one leg? It would be Wade Morgan with a .45 slug in his brain. Pity for the broken man on the bunk filled the boy's heart. Wade, who could turn cartwheels and flips with the ease of an acrobat. Wade, who could ride anything they could get into a corral. Wade, who could whip a roomful of hard men. Wade, who would sit up all night nursing a sick dog or cat. Devil-be-damned, happy-go-lucky Wade Morgan. The outlaw trail and Yuma had broken him. This man on the bunk was an old man, white of hair, weak, smashed. Only his courage was unscarred. A man's courage is a precious thing, too splendid to be marred by defeat and bitterness. It burned, like a consuming flame, in the heart of Wade Morgan. Whatever end Fate had marked out for this man, he would meet it without compromise. Wade Morgan would die game. To die game—that was the one and only prize that lay at the end of the outlaw trail. A courageous death. Let men say what they would of him, they would not dare malign the manner of his passing. By dying game the outlaw claims the right of respect from his enemies. And he retains caste among his kind.

Joe, sitting there in the cabin, somehow knew those things. He saw, there on the log walls and on the heavy plank door, the rudely carved names of men who had stopped there for an hour or a week or a winter. Names of men whose deeds of outlawry were sung in cow-land saga. Names of living men who made up the human wolf pack. Names of other men who had died with their boots on and their guns smoking. Bits of penciled verse. Dates. Crude pictures of men and horses. Jocular and profane bits that touched on the characters of certain law officers. And certain messages left by men who had ridden on, left to be read and understood by some comrade who would stop there. Joe read these bits of carvings and penciled messages and rhymes. It was like learning a first lesson in outlawry. Perhaps, because he was a true son of an outlaw, he understood the hearts of the men who had left these scraps of inscriptions. There was a date: XMAS 1895. Bill and Buck. Bull Edwards and Buck Buell. Here, in this cabin, they had made their last stand. A vigilante crowd had hung their bullet-drilled bodies to that big cottonwood down on the river. Later, years later, those well-meaning but stupid vigilantes learned they had hung the wrong men. Tragedy there. Another bit of jackknife artistry, neatly done but unfinished. Rawhi . . . Rawhide Bob. An old enemy and Rawhide Bob had shot it out in this cabin. Their unmarked graves within a stone's throw of where they had jerked their last triggers.

If you come this way, Sim Patchen, mark a date under this. I'll meet you here and show you how to make a coyote run.

WADE MORGAN.

There was no date beneath this bit of foolish bravado. The gesture was typical of the man who now lay there on the bunk, broken in body, muttering in delirium. There was a drawing of a man being piled by a pitching horse. There was a well executed picture of a woman's profile. Another depicted a hanging. There was written, in a beautiful Spencerian hand, a poem about Zebra Dun. Pete Davenport of the Circle-C was its author. There were the names of Johnnie and Lonie Curry, brothers of the Kid, both dead now. And on the outer side of the door some unnamed outlaw had burned an inscription with a running iron:

Fools Cabin

Wade Morgan stirred uneasily and opened his eyes. Their burning gaze fixed on the face of Joe.

"I'd sooner be dead than be yore kind of a sheriff, Patchen."

Then his eyes shifted his mad gaze to the window. He tried to wrench free of the ropes that held him. He thought he was back in a Yuma cell, being strung up by the thumbs with only his toes touching the filthy floor. He was cursing his jailor.

Joe listened, the color drained from his lips. It was rather horrible to hear a man curse like that and suffer so terribly. Joe had heard of Yuma—its heat and filth and punishments. The toughest pen in the United States, down on the Mexican border. Heat that killed. Nights with a chill that bit through sweat-caked skin and into the marrow of a man's bones. Cells that held men dying of the dread prison plague, locked in with well men who were fated to contract the highly contagious disease. Mexicans and Indians and niggers and white men. They gave a man five years to live at Yuma, so the outlaws claimed. Solitary at Yuma was a chamber of horrors. Black, stifling, crawling with vermin. Joe saw Yuma through the delirious ravings of his father. Saw the price paid for riding the outlaw trail. Saw what it did to the souls of men born and reared on the open range where a man's roof was the stars and there were no walls. . . .

He tried to break through Wade's delirium and bring back sanity to the wounded man's brain. But his efforts were in vain.

Chapter Six

SO-LONG, PARDNER

THAT afternoon one of the outlaws rode up and stayed to supper with Joe. He was a young man, not much older than Joe. He had blue eyes and a blunt sunburned nose that was peeling. He wore two six-shooters and walked with a limp. Joe noticed that he kept watching the wooded ridges of the box cañon. Restless as some animal. He played the harmonica and whistled the "Dying Cowboy." He told Joe that he had killed three men and expected to kill a few more before he died. There was a hard, bitter look sometimes, in his blue eyes. He was a preacher's son, but didn't believe in God.

"If there's a God, why is there cripples that crawl in the dirt? Why does he let cattle starve and die off of a hard winter? What good on earth is rattlesnakes and tarant'lars? When a man dies, he's dead and rots there. Heaven? Hell!"

Joe listened in silence. He had an idea that this young outlaw was repeating words voiced by some older, more embittered man. Joe believed in God and a hereafter but he had the wisdom to avoid argument because they never won a man anything in the long run.

The blue-eyed youth said for Joe to call him Cotton Top. He let Joe do the cooking and wash the dishes. He sat in the doorway, his restless eyes always hunting for some moving thing up on the cañon ridges. He smoked too many cigarettes and every other word was a profane one. Joe thought Cotton Top talked too much with his mouth and wondered why the seasoned outlaws let him trail with them. He did not know that this blue-eyed, mouthy youth had another side—a sinister, merciless, cool-brained side; that Cotton Top's job was to hold the horses of the others. A job he carried out with cool efficiency in spite of hailing bullets. This fit of talking was reaction, a sort of hysteria caused from pulled, scraped nerves. Once, when a twig snapped out there in the dusk, Cotton Top twisted from the doorway with the speed and agility of a cougar. He crouched behind the door, his guns naked, his blue eyes slitted. Cotton Top put away his guns and laughed a little too loudly. Nerves. He looked across the room at Joe who stood beside his father's bunk. Wade's .45 was in Joe's hand, and he was smiling crookedly with tightly pulled lips. Cotton Top nodded approval.

"Wish you'd join up with us, Joe. Yo're more my age. The others are older. I bet you'd do battle all right."

Joe put up the gun and went back to his dishes. Wade had dropped off into a dead sleep. Cotton Top amused himself by throwing bits of food to a pair of scolding, bold-mannered magpies.

Joe was a little relieved when Cotton Top got his horse and rode away with a careless, "So-long, pardner. See yuh later."

Joe never saw him again. Cotton Top was killed a month or so later in a New Mexico gambling house. True to his promise, he took three men with him into eternity. His last, blood-flecked racking breath had carried the name of God. Whether in blasphemy or prayer, none but Cotton Top and his Maker could ever know.

Joe, alone once more with his father, felt like a person suddenly exiled to another world. He felt strange, as if he were gripped by some nightmare. Yet, to his own bewilderment, he fitted into this life without effort.

He was glad when Long Bob and Doc Steele rode up out of the night. Doc looked at Joe intently, his keen eyes reading much of what stirred in the boy's blood. For Joe looked white under his tanned skin, and his eyes were too bright and unreal.

Doc dressed Wade's leg. Long Bob helped him. They made Joe sit outside the cabin. And when the leg was dressed, Doc talked to Bob in an undertone.

"This is no place for the lad, Bob. He's too highly strung. He's seen and heard too much already. He goes back with me to-night if we have to tie him in his saddle. It's wrong, wrong as hell to let him stay. Wade has one chance in a thousand to pull through, and there aren't many men I'd give that one chance to, understand. Wade Morgan is tough and in spite of his physical condition, he had a lot of reserve. He'll be needing every atom of it these next days. Any sane surgeon would amputate, but—" Doc's eyes rested on the big .45 on the shelf and Long Bob nodded. "So we'll do what we can, Bob, all that's humanly possible to save the leg and save Wade's life. But it's going to be hell for him and hell for the man that's nursing him."

The two men had been standing near the bunk, their backs half turned to the wounded outlaw. A brittle laugh from the bunk brought them around. Wade Morgan's eyes were open and there was a queer expression on his face.

"So it's a thousand to one shot in the devil's favor, is it?" Wade croaked huskily. "Well, that's good enough for me, boys. How about a little drink, Doc?"

Doc strode to the water bucket and dipped out a cup ful of the cold spring water. "You're on the Injun list for a while Wade. No booze. Drink hearty." He held the cup to Wade': fever-dried lips. Wade grinned and drank.

"Sounds silly as hell, boys, but I was dreamin' that little Joe had bin here."

"Joe has bin takin' care of yuh, Wade," said Long Bob "He's outside now. I'll fetch him in."

Joe came in at Bob's summons. Pride shone in the outlaw': eyes as he gripped the boy's hand.

"Gosh, Joe, you've done growed up, ain't yuh? A growed man." He stared at his son and seemed unable to say anything more. His bloodshot eyes softened and he dropped Joe's hand confusedly.

Joe, too, seemed at loss for words. They just looked at one another.

"Does Long Bob still call yuh Little Britches, Joe?" he finally broke a silence that was becoming painful.

"Sometimes," Joe grinned a little.

"I'm glad you come, Joe. Doc says I'll probably kick the bucket, but I don't reckon I will. But in case he's right, I'm glad I seen yuh. I'm in a bad shape, right now, and I'm kinda sorry yuh had to see me like this, savvy. And yo're a-goin' home with Doc. Don't come back, Joe. And don't ever git it into yore head to do what I done. In this game, even if yuh win, yuh lose. And fer every real man yuh meet, there's a hundred snakes. . . . Doin' good in school, Joe?"

"I'm going to a military school back east."

"The hell! Yuh ain't gonna be a soldier, are yuh, Joe?"

"Gosh, no. I'm studying law, or I will be, when I enter college next year."

"Law?" Wade's forehead wrinkled quizzically. "Law, Joe?"

"Doc and Almanac and I decided on that. I like it."

Wade's tight-lipped mouth twisted at one corner. "Law! Laws are made for rich men. For the railroads. They make the laws and when a poor man busts one, he goes to the pen. They buy the judge and the jury. There ain't a damn law in this country that a rich man can't buy if he's rich and wears a stiff collar. Damn the law. I'd sooner see yuh herdin' sheep. You, Doc, what are you and that old fool of an Almanac a-tryin' to do to the kid?"

"Trying to make a man out of him, Wade. Keep your shirt tail tucked in your pants. This country needs men like Joe that are honest. Do you think any man's dirty money will ever buy that lad? Wade Morgan, you're a damned fool. Now shut up and take it quiet or I'll have Bob rap you across that bone head with a gun barrel. Joe's going to be a real man some day. Montana will never be ashamed of Joe Morgan. And when he sits on the bench as Judge of the Supreme Court, there won't be enough money in the country to bribe him. Are you licked, you darned idiot?"

The sneer left Wade Morgan's mouth. "I'll take 'er back, Joe. Doc savvies the burro. I hope tuh see yuh governor some day. Mabby so you'd pardon some of yore old man friends." He turned to Doc Steele, who had caught the undertone of bitterness in the broken outlaw's words.

"Look over there in them overalls, Doc. Keep what yuh find in 'em."

"Do you think for one damned second, Wade, that I'm doing this for money?"

"No, but you might as well have it. There's better than ten thousand there. If I live, it'll go fer houses and lots. Sportin' houses and lots of redeye whisky."

"I don't need it, Wade. You might."

"Then it's yourn, Bob. Blow it or lay it aside fer Joe's schoolin'." Again the pain-parched mouth twisted. "Wouldn't that be a hell of a joke? Outlaw money educatin' a future judge. A hell of a joke, I'd say."

He broke into a rattling laugh that ended in a coughing spell. Doc gripped Joe's arm. "Don't mind him, lad, he's sick." Joe nodded and forced a smile.

Doc made Wade take a couple of capsules. When he had dropped off to sleep the three left. Joe paused in the doorway for a last look at the man who was his father. There was a hard lump in the boy's throat that ached.

"Little Britches," Wade muttered in his sleep. "Done growed up, ain't yuh, little Joe?" And a wistful pride in the husky voice stung Joe's eyes with tears.

Up past the head of the bad-lands Long Bob untied Doc's blindfold. Joe and Doc rode on. Long Bob went back to stay with the sick man. To stay until Wade Morgan either got well —or asked for the colt .45 up on the shelf.

At the Clanton ranch, a heated argument was being waged. Tug and Tim had discovered the cabin. They had seen Joe there. They were all for notifying Sim Patchen. Bill Clanton favored the idea. The snuff-dipping Ma Clanton lashed them with profane abuse.

"Wait. Wait, you sheep-headed half-wits! Damn yore damn

43

eyes, wait!" Her whisky-cracked voice shrilled to a thin screech
They were afraid of her and her butcher knife and her double
bitted ax.

"God, ain't we waited six years? Wait fer what?" snarled
Bill.

"Yeah," echoed the burly sons, "what in hell we waitin' fer?

"Wade Morgan's at that cabin, hurt er sick." Bill lowered
his voice to a whisper. "There's ten thousand dollars on 'im.

"Yes, you damn old fool, an' nobody by the name o' Clanton
'd ever sight a red penny of it by the time Sim Patchen an
his men got done splittin' it. All you'd git would be a dose u
gun lead. Bob Burch'd kill yuh. Wait yuh fools."

The old hag's voice dropped to a whisper. "If yuh gott
know, yo're waitin' fer Joe Morgan an' Amy Steele."

"Joe Morgan?"

"That's it," cackled the woman, "Joe Morgan. We'll fix 'i
some day. Some day, when they've got done makin' a dude out
him. And that gal of Steele's!" She spat into the fire, her fac
twitching. "When we git done with 'er, she'll be willin' to marr
anybody. Even one of you two blockheads. Don't I know wha
Steele's a-plannin'? Fixin' Joe Morgan so's he'll be fit fer th
Steele brat. Wait! Wait, you fools!"

Because they feared her, and because their crime-warpe
minds dwelt upon her promise, Bill Clanton and his two son
waited. And Sim Patchen was not given the chance to collec
the ten thousand dollars on the life of Wade Morgan.

Almost a month later, Long Bob Burch came home. He tol
Hattie and Almanac and Joe that Wade had hit the trail fc
the Wind River country over in Wyoming. His leg, thanks t
God and Doc Steele and his own tough courage, had healec
So Wade had taken his guns and ridden away to join the drift
ing members of the Wild Bunch. A gaunt, cold-eyed, thir
lipped replica of the old laughing Wade; a white-haired, wit
a cough and a heart that was bitter as gall, Wade Morgan wa
all killer now.

Chapter Seven

PARADE

DOC STEELE helped Joe nail the neatly printed sign abov
the door of the log cabin that served as an office for the youn
lawyer fresh from his university: "JOE MORGAN, ATTORNEY-A
LAW." Directly across the street was the saloon in which Wac

44

Morgan had killed Shotgun Riley. Its doorway and two big windows were packed with faces. Out in front of the saloon stood Bull Mitchell, a derisive grin on his heavy face. With him stood Sim Patchen and Peg Leg Love. Some miners and cow-punchers, a couple of bleary-eyed sheepherders, a sprinkling of tin-horn gamblers and a white-aproned bartender made up the crowd that watched the sign being tacked down above the door of the log cabin. Other citizens and drifters ambled with curious step, up the one street of Pay Dirt.

With Joe and Doc Steele were Almanac, Hattie, Mrs. Steele and Amy. Amy, on the verge of womanhood, had put on her best frock. He mother and Joe's mother had brought along large lunch baskets.

Long Bob now rode up the street with a group of cow-punchers from the round-up camp below town. Behind their careless banter lay a barely perceptible vigilance. They had come to Pay Dirt to celebrate Joe Morgan's new venture, and to see that Bull Mitchell did not try any rough tactics to discourage Joe.

"If it'll do any good, Bob," said a lanky Texan, "I'll shoot up Mitchell's saloon and stand trial with Joe fer my law sharp. It'll start him off right." He meant it, but Long Bob discouraged the idea.

The town had grown these past years, grown beyond the brawny reach of Bull Mitchell. Outside capital had come in. There were two new mills up the gulch. New mines were work-ing three eight-hour shifts. There was a post-office, a new mercantile store, two restaurants, an assay office, a schoolhouse and three saloons besides the old Shotgun Riley place. The name of the town was changed from Shotgun Gulch to Pay Dirt. Some of the mining officials had brought along their wives and families, thus lending an air of respectability to the place whose only women had been those of the dance halls and the red-curtained cabins in Whisky Gulch. The town was no longer Bull Mitchell's town. Opposed to his high-handed ruling that was backed by Peg Leg Love and Sim Patchen, there had come into being a Vigilance Committee. This latter crowd was made up of sober-minded citizens who frowned on promiscuous killings and rowdyism. If Bull Mitchell and his crowd failed to recognize the fact that their heyday of red power was on the wane, they would not openly admit it. They held to their own side of the street that had become a sort of deadline. And there was no man of sufficient boldness among the more decent ele-ment that dared bring their rulings past that deadline. And so Pay Dirt was now divided. And Bull Mitchell's faction was the stronger because Bull was a born leader and a strong leader and he had Sim Patchen behind him.

Long Bob and the cowpunchers put up their horses at the new barn. They paused at the Longhorn Bar for a drink. The Longhorn was the saloon favored by the cow-men.

Tex Buford, owner and bartender at the Longhorn, greeted them warmly. Tex had been a cowman himself.

"So the boy's settin' up his shingle here in Pay Dirt, Bob? Well, I reckon it's up to us to make him feel he's among home folks. Doc let it out that Joe was a-comin' here. Here yuh are, cowboys." He began passing across the bar a miscellaneous collection of tin pans.

"I'm shy on drum sticks, boys. Use yore hog laigs." Tex stepped from behind the bar with a brass horn of some description. He was a huge man and he loomed up at the head of the tin-pan drum corps that marched grandly up the street, six-shooters for drum sticks, spurs jingling. The whistles at the Lost Lode and Adeline mines began shrilling. From the opposite end of the street, where they had gathered at the Miner's Home Bar, a khaki and a hobnailed parade came marching. Shift bosses, engineers, muckers. A little drunk but in a festive mood. The two delegations met in front of Joe's cabin. Almanac, still sober, beamed as if this ovation was in honor of him. Doc Steele gripped Joe's arm. The women were flushed with excitement. Joe looked confused and a little frightened.

The parade halted. Bull Mitchell's gang looked on sourly, but made no move to break up the celebration. They were calling on Joe for a speech. They lifted him up on top of some boxes that held his books and office equipment. Joe, a little white from the shock of it all, his eyes bright with emotion, cleared his throat which seemed awfully tight and aching.

"I didn't expect anything like this," he told them, his voice a trifle husky, "and it's mighty hard to find the right sort of words to thank you. I'm more proud to-day than I've ever been in my life, I reckon. It sorts of does something to a man's heart when he gets the brand of homecoming that you folks are giving me. So if I can't seem to put it all in words, I want you to know that it's because I'm too dog-goned happy to even think clearly.

"I picked Pay Dirt because I was born near here and I want to live here. I believe that there is room here for an attorney." Joe paused. From his improvised platform he looked across the heads of his friends and toward Bull Mitchell and his crowd. Joe smiled a little and his shoulders squared.

"It won't be any bed of roses for me, here in Pay Dirt. In

fact, I've been warned to stay clear of this town. But I came in spite of that warning. I'm here. I'll stay here and fight. I may be carried out feet first. But no man nor group of men can make me run out of Pay Dirt. I have no chip on my shoulder. I don't pack a gun. I'm no long-maned reformer. But if I can help bring the law into Pay Dirt, I'll feel more than repaid for coming back here.

"My name is Joe Morgan. My father is Wade Morgan. A man called Shotgun Riley sent him out on the outlaw trail. You folks all know the story You know what I'm up against and you're wondering how I'll meet that issue. The only way I can tell you is to stay here and play my string out. I surely hope none of you will ever regret to-day when you made me feel welcome here. I thank you."

Joe Morgan leaped lightly to the ground. The tin-pan corps set up a wild din. Men shook Joe's hand until his arm ached. Then they all marched over to the schoolhouse where the women of the town had set long tables covered with the sort of repast that one never finds beyond the wide borderline of the open country. Pay Dirt thus declared its holiday in honor of Joe Morgan. Men knew that Joe Morgan represented the law. Law had come to Pay Dirt.

If Bull Mitchell realized the danger that now came to further threaten his régime, he hid that knowledge from his cohorts. He set up rounds of free drinks His piano thumper and fiddler sweat profusely. The red-lipped women of his dance hall and his houses in Whisky Gulch, danced unsteadily with drunken, sweat-fouled partners whose hob-nails bit into the pine floor and occasionally crushed a silken instep.

The street was deserted save for some drunken reveler who had stayed outside for air. Up this dusty street now came a laden spring wagon. To the wagon was hitched a leg-weary team of livery horses. A breed boy held the lines. Beside him sat a lanky, lean-jawed man dressed in city clothes. His bright greenish eyes were aided by a pair of black-rimmed glasses. His sardonic mouth smiled. On the seat beside him was an almost empty bottle of Scotch whisky But if the man was drunk, he had a knack of concealing it. His long, bony forefinger pointed to an empty cabin next to Joe Morgan's. His keen eyes passed from Joe's new sign to the empty cabin alongside the new law office.

"That domicile will do nicely, Nicodemus," he said in a voice that in spite of its flat tone held a coloring of queer humor. "We'll unload right next to the office of Joe Morgan, Attorney-at-Law."

"Huh?" The breed boy eyed his companion uneasily, as if he were sure that he spoke to a man afflicted with some form of insanity.

Gravely the tall man repeated his words in Spanish, then in some Scandinavian tongue, trimming it with a few profane bits of German and French.

"In other words, my boy, get out of the carriage and get under some of the stuff in the wagon. And if you drop anything I'll borrow a gun and shoot you to small bits which I'll make you eat raw and without salt. . . . Ah! Greetings of the season, friend!"

He spoke the latter words to Joe Morgan who had come back to his brand-new office to get some cigars Almanac had left there.

Joe, still flushed from excitement, eyed the stranger with friendly, mildly quizzical eyes. The tall, astonishingly thin man removed a Panama hat and bowed. His head was covered with closely cut wavy hair that was white as snow. The hand he held out was bony and white and well-kept.

"If I should be granted but one guess," he said, "I'd say that I had the honor of meeting Joe Morgan, Attorney-at-Law. Upon you I know I now inflict the pain of your knowing Peter Bartholomew Smyth. S, as in souse; M, as in Martini; Y, as in Yin rickey, Swedishly speaking; T, as you find it in tankard; H, for halleluja, or have this one on me." He reached for his bottle and solemnly uncorked it. "I see we're to be next-door neighbors. Drink hearty."

Joe lifted the bottle and took a small drink. Peter Bartholomew Smyth smiled and finished the bottle, handing the empty container to the gaping breed.

"You may call me Pete, Joe. I'm editor of the Pay Dirt *Assay*. It springs into being to-morrow, if the liquor hereabouts is good and not too plentiful. I give you my history in brief. I was sent out from the *World* to cover the Ketchell fight in Butte. I must have taken the odd drink too many. When I awoke, the fight had been over for a week. I wired New York asking them if I had covered the assignment to their satisfaction, and nonchalantly adding that I was strapped and needed a hundred berries. I wired collect. So did the editor. His was a message sublime in its simplicity. 'When you sober up,' says he, 'read this. Stop. You were fired a week ago. Period.'

"I left Butte. Stopped at Chinook to hunt up an old classmate at school. Found out he was doing a ten-year stretch at Deer Lodge for selling some sucker a salted mine. I took my last fin and ran it up to fifty with a pair of gallopers Then I sat me down in a game of stud Finding I had fallen among smart companions, I did, perforce, as one does under such trying conditions In words of one syllable, Pete Smyth, Y, as in yegg, became likewise smart. I left them the next morning with a fat roll of Uncle's yellow-backed currency, a beautiful hangover, and the sole ownership of a non-self-supporting newspaper Some one had mentioned Pay Dirt The name hung among the cobwebs of my attic I hired this team and conveyance, loaded my newly acquired press, and set forth upon my pilgrimage The name of Pay Dirt had quite overpowered me So here I am, my last quart gone the way of many others, a stranger among strangers When sober, I never drink When under the influence, I will tackle anything from paint-remover to pain-killer Drunk or sober you will find me as you now see me, a genial soul in quest of companionship and the next drink Never loan me money Never attempt to reform me. If I ever bore you, tell me Unless my eyes betray me, that domicile down the street bears a familiar sign Thirst gripes me Let's imbibe and if you'll allow me, I'll do the buying Oh, yes It quite slipped my mind By way of accomplishments and bar-room tricks, I recite 'Gunga Din' backwards with an introduction in the Yiddish "

Smyth walked without the hint of a stagger His enunciation was clear Yet Joe knew that the man was drunk. He accompanied him to Tex Buford's saloon and introduced him to the cowpunchers who lined the bar The lanky newspaperman, for all his city ways, won them over in no time He had been, so it seemed, in every remote corner of the world He had the gift of fitting into any sort of company Joe Morgan was beginning to like him

For all his odd manners and flippancy, there was something pathetic behind those bright greenish eyes Noticing the manner in which Pete Smyth attacked the free lunch, Joe made him accompany him back to the schoolhouse Nor did he regret that move Smyth had the manners of a Don Not a woman there even guessed that Pete Smyth was drunk Later, before the dance that night, as Joe and some others helped unload the printing press, Smyth confessed that he hadn't eaten a decent meal in four or five days

So began a friendship that was to endure through the hard years that lay in wait for Joe Morgan, Attorney-at-Law

Chapter Eight

THE BELLE OF PAY DIRT

BULL MITCHELL was drunk.

Once or twice during each year Bull got on a drunk that would last about a week. Even his friends, or to be more exact those who claimed to be his friends—Pete Smyth had not yet coined that expression "hired friends"—even those friends hated to be near the self-styled boss of Pay Dirt when he got drunk because he was treacherous and dangerous. His strength was terrible, his whisky-crazed brain was cunning and ugly. He fought with fists, feet, teeth and any weapon that came handy

"Seems like there's a dance going on at the schoolhouse,' he told the gang at the saloon. "They're giving it for young Morgan. Later on this evenin', we'll take our girls and join 'em. They forgot to send us invitations but I'll see to it that we git in. Bull Mitchell's the boss of this camp."

No man or woman there disputed the big man's word. They feared his terrible strength and brutality. He had broken men who dared dispute his slightest wishes. He had tortured women who refused his brutal advances. The tin-eared, broken-nosed one-eyed thug who now served drinks had tasted of Bull Mitchell's punishment. Bull had gouged out his other eye in a fight that lasted nearly two hours. And Casey—that was the bartender's name—had been a tough heavyweight with a score of ring victories to his credit. Bull had fought him with bare fists and beaten him down to a bloody, whimpering pulp. Then he had hired Casey.

Among the women was an olive-skinned girl known as Black Diamond. Time had been when she had been strikingly beautiful in a dark-eyed, red-lipped, creamy-bodied, statuesque way. But liquor and Bull Mitchell's fists had blurred her handsomeness. She had grown heavy. There was an ugly twist to the full red mouth. She was Bull Mitchell's queen and she ruled the dance-hall girls with a devilish, shrewish temper and her diamond-bedecked hands were like tiger's paws—velvet-smooth, quick-striking. A thin-bladed knife and a blacksnake were her pet weapons.

Once, years before, she had fought Bull Mitchell with those weapons and had lost only when his big hairy fists had beaten her senseless. When she was able to crawl about she had nursed

Bull Mitchell back to health, for he was a mass of cuts and welts. She loved this brute with all the power of her strange heart. And she had a queer sort of power over him not unlike an uncanny and weird sorcery.

The dance-hall girls hated her, feared her, waited on her, and fought among themselves for her favor. One alone among them openly defied her. That one was a small-statured, auburn-haired, gray-eyed girl who dealt faro bank and sometimes presided at the black-jack and poker tables. She had a snub little nose, a little clean-chiseled jaw, a frank smile and a ready wit that served her well. She always carried a small-calibered pistol and knew how to use it. Her name was Kit Kavanaugh and her father had been one of the greatest gamblers that ever marked a deck. Among the fraternity he was remembered as The Deacon. It was said that he had killed eighteen men in fair fight before he finally died of blood poisoning from a scratch on his thumb. Deacon Kavanaugh had always taken his motherless daughter with him—from Mexico City to Nome, from New Orleans and Hot Springs to 'Frisco and Butte, Reno, Tombstone, and working the boats along the Mississippi. He had taught her every card trick known and as a sideline he had taught Kit virtue. Somehow Kit Kavanaugh had acquired an education. Men liked Kit Kavanaugh even after she let them know that she was not for sale. Women trusted her and told her their troubles. So did men. And her Irish heart seemed always big enough to hold it all.

Kit Kavanaugh had been with Mitchell almost a year. She had made him and herself a lot of money during that year. The second night she worked for him, she told Bull that if ever he laid a hand on her she would kill him. "And that goes for the queen, Mitchell. Try any of your little games on me, Black Diamond, and you'll be kissin' the devil good mornin'."

Kit Kavanaugh lived alone in a large log cabin up near the mine superintendent's house. She had sought no favors from the decent women of the town. She furnished her cabin with beautiful furniture and did all her own housework and cooking. Sometimes, when she sat at the baby grand piano in her front room and played, those passing would stop and listen in awed silence. No man ever went hungry in Pay Dirt if Kit Kavanaugh knew it. Every youngster in town worshipped her. Not at first, because their mothers forbade them to go near her.

Then came the evening when the mine superintendent's two youngsters got hold of a box of matches. Their parents were away. The house, a frame building, was a mass of flames when the neighbors discovered the fire. And from inside those four

walls of red flames came the terrified screams of the two chi
dren.

Men and women stood about, white-faced and helpless. The
a red-haired girl in hiking clothes had scrambled through th
fringe of helpless men. Without a second's pause she had foug
her way into the house. Some minutes later she staggered ot
again, the children, wrapped in blankets, in her arms. Her ow
clothes were afire, her face blistered, her red hair badly singe
But she had taken the family into her home until they coul
find another. After that the women called on her and the
children spent half their time at Kit's cabin.

To-night Kit was dressed in a simple, but Paris-made froc
of dull green. Her hair, the color of burnished copper, lay i
thick coils against the ivory white of her neck. Her gray eye
were soft and her mind seemed to be on other things beside
the cards.

The gambling was weak and insipid. Kit Kavanaugh slippe
out of the place and into the night. Without an escort, sh
walked up the gulch toward the schoolhouse. She was hummin
a little Irish song and her gray eyes were fixed on the stars—
because that afternoon, Kit Kavanaugh had met the only ma
that had ever made her heart skip a beat. That man was youn
Joe Morgan.

"I'm twenty," she said softly to her reflection in her mirro
when she had gone home to supper, "and he's all of twenty-tw
and looks a bit older. Kit, old trouper, it's time you quit th
hurdy-gurdy honkey-tonk life and begin' sewin' buttons on th
shirts of a decent, clean boy like Joe Morgan."

On the way through the soft summer night she let a tin
scowl mar the soft ivory above the level gray eyes. She ha
also met Amy Steele that day. She had, with her eyes that ha
seen life as few girls see it, read the heart of Amy Steele. Am
loved Joe Morgan.

"But love's an open game and the sky's the limit, accordir
to Hoyle or Shakespeare or some smart boy. I've found my ma
and I'll fight to make him care for me. I can give him thing
that Amy Steele can never give a man because she don't knov
women. She hasn't lived with men all her life and studied 'em
She wouldn't know what to do when he was blue or beaten o
drunk or wanter to fight. She wouldn't be waitin' on him an
bringin' him his pipe and slippers and settin' a table with hi
kind of food. She wouldn't know how to hold him if some woma
tried to steal him. She's a nice, sweet, wholesome kid, but she'
not the woman for that boy. He's Wade Morgan's son and Wad
Morgan went bad. Supposin' the breaks come bad and Joe i

tempted to turn bad? Could that kid hold him? Not in a million years."

She halted on the steps outside the schoolhouse. A group of men stood in the shadows smoking. They had not noticed her.

"Would there be," she called lightly, "a gallant hero among you who would be so generous as to loan a silly girl the use of a handkerchief to wipe half the red dust of Pay Dirt from a nice new pair of slippers?"

Before any of them could offer aid, a tall, angular man stepped forward. In his hand was a spotless white linen handkerchief. The light from inside fell on the girl and the man.

"It may be that last drink I partook of," said the man, "that so plays tricks with my eyes. But I'm a pigtailed Chinaman if you aren't the daughter of a dear old friend of my youth."

"Pete!" gasped Kit Kavanaugh. "Peter Bartholomew Smyth! Y, as in Yodel, to quote the Alpine."

"Kit, you're the same old knockout. Shall I lay my heart at your feet here or—"

Kit took his two hands, gripped them hard, and kissed him on top of his snow-white hair. The man in the shadows looked on in grinning bewilderment.

"How long have you been on this bender, Pete?" she asked in a low tone. "Tell mother the truth."

"Less than a month, Kitten."

"I'm going to dance now, Pete. My cabin is the second one up the gulch from here. I'm going home at twelve and I expect to find you waiting there. There's a bottle of decent whisky in the cupboard over the fireplace. There's cold chicken and lettuce and tomatoes and lots more grub in the cooler. Likewise a spare bedroom. I'll get a wire off to Kelly in the mornin'."

"I've already wired Kelly," smiled Pete Smyth. "And received a reply from the big bum. I'm fired."

"For the eleventh time," nodded Kit, "but he'll take you back, Pete."

"But I don't care about going back, Kitten. You are now conversing with no menial subject at the beck and call of uncouth editors with the hearts of pig-iron. Have you ever read the Pay Dirt *Assay?* No? Nor has anyone. But by this time next week it will be read hither and yon, in the humble huts of peasants and in the palaces of kings. And it is none other than I, Peter Bartholomew Smyth, Y as in Ukulele, who is father of that brain-child that shall journey across the continent and bring cheer and light into the dark corners of the earth. I need a society editor. You're it, Kitten. I already have acquired a columnist of merit, a newborn genius. His name is Almanac Jones."

Kneeling, he carefully dusted Kit's slippers and stood aside wit
a bow. "On with the dance, let joy be unrefined."

There were tears in Kit Kavanaugh's eyes as she smiled a
him and went inside. She paused a moment to whisper some
thing in the ear of Long Bob Burch. Bob nodded grimly an
went outside.

"We're due to have some uninvited company, boys," he tol
the cowpunchers. "Bull Mitchell's comin' over here to bust u
the dance."

Chapter Nine

FIGHT

AT HALF past eleven o'clock, a lone horseman left the Shotgu
Riley Saloon and rode down the street and out of town. Tha
rider was Sim Patchen, deputy sheriff of Pay Dirt. Patchen wa
giving Pay Dirst into the keeping of his boss, Bull Mitchell. Th
move, it must be said for Sim Pathen, was not voluntary. Hi
protests had been beaten down by Bull's menacing eyes. "Gi
out town, Sim. Come back tomorrow." And Sim Patchen ha
not sufficient courage to disobey.

When Bill Clanton, watching from the saloon doorway, cam
back in and whispered to Bull that Sim had quit town and Pe
Leg had vanished, the burly boss of Pay Dirt bellowed for si
lence and made a short speech.

"Feller citizens, 'I'm the biggest tax-payer in camp. Me an
Riley put our coin in here and built up a town. Now these dam
tin-bills is a-tryin' to run me out. That schoolhouse is as mucl
ours as it is theirs. Our money helped build it. None of use ha
any kids benefitin' from it. Are we gonna be bluffed by a pack o
wolves like them? Are we gonna let 'em say they scared us out?'

"Not by a darn sight, Bull!" roared bill Clanton, who was hal
drunk. Bill had been in town two days. He'd come in with
load of wood and two dressed beeves. The bartender, the poke
table, and a dance-hall girl had painlessly extracted his money
Bull Mitchell had advanced Bill Clanton another hundred dollar
and taken a mortgage on his team and wagon. That hundred wa
almost gone. Bill Clanton was afraid to go home.

"Do what I tell yuh, Clanton, and I'll square yuh with yor
old woman."

So Bill Clanton, drunk and in a desperate mood, was backin
Bull Mitchell's game. So were several other cold-eyed gents Bul

kept on his payroll. These latter drank sparingly and had a tough name. Two of them had notches on their guns.

"Lead us to 'em, Bull!"

"Then grab yore pardners for the grand march!" Bull set the pace, Black Diamond at his side. Bill Clanton's lee-like lady followed suit. Others did likewise. About fifteen couples in all—the women hiding their reluctance behind shrill laughter, the men with their hands on their guns. Bull Mitchell looked at the throng that circled the dance floor back of the gambling layouts.

"Where's Kit Kavanaugh?" he barked. Casey shrugged his thick shoulders and handed Bull a folded note. Bull opened it.

Go buy a dictionary and look up the meaning of the word Nauseate. That's what your joint does to me. I've cashed in my last chips here.

Black Diamond, reading over Bull's shoulder, laughed shortly. Bull was white with fury He swung around, his fist clenched. Black Diamond sneered at him.

"Don't swing on me, Bull, or I'll cut your heart out and send it to that red-headed wench for a keepsake. Think I'm blind? Think I couldn't see you was stuck on her? Good thing for you and her both that she took the air." Her voice was a low, husky whisper and her dark eyes were red with hate. "Buy this mob a drink, then we'll take in the dance."

It was an ugly, dangerous mob that made their way up the street to the dance at the schoolhouse. They paused, just outside. Then Bull Mitchell and his fighting queen marched up the steps, the others following. There was a cloakroom at the entrance. The door between the cloakroom and the dance floor was closed. From the other side of the closed door came the sound of fiddle and accordion playing "Hell Among the Yearlings." A caller was barking his, "Ladies in the center and four hands 'round!" There was laughter and the scraping of feet. The cloakroom itself was dark. Its walls were hung with wraps. There was the faint odor of tobacco smoke and perfume. Bull hesitated. A voice came out of the darkness.

"You're making a bad mistake, Mitchell."

"What yuh say?" rasped Mitchell. "Who says so?"

"Joe Morgan."

"Who else with yuh?"

"Nobody. I'm in here alone. But just on the other side of this door are some friends of mine, Mitchell, that will back up my play. You and your drunken friends aren't wanted here."

"Git the windy brat, Bull." It was Bill Clanton's voice.

"I'm not packing a gun, Mitchell," came Joe Morgan's voice. "If you shoot, it'll be murder. But if you'll step across the road, I'll fight you with my hands."

"Yuh will, huh? Listen, I'll call that bet. Step out." Bull shoved his way outside, pushing his followers back down the steps. Joe Morgan followed behind the crowd. From out of the shadows alongside the building came two men with lanterns. One of these was Almanac Jones, the other was Long Bob Burch. Joe joined them.

"I tell yuh, Joe," said Bob uneasily, "that big jasper'll kill yuh. Gawd, he outweighs yuh fifty popnds."

"It's my scrap, Bob."

Almanac said nothing. There was a grin on his bearded mouth and his old white-handled gun was shoved down in the waist-band of his overalls within quick reach of his gnarled hand. His eyes kept glancing toward a clump of willows that flanked the creek.

Bull Mitchell led the way to a secluded spot across the road that led down from the mills. The crowd with him formed a circle. The lanterns were hung from the low branches of trees, shedding a yellow light across the cleared space. Bull Mitchell was shedding his gun belt with a show of swaggering bravado. He ripped off his flannel shirt and undershirt. Across the white flesh under his shoulder was an ugly red scar. Joe Morgan's bullet had made that years before.

Joe peeled off his coat and shirt, looked at it and grinned. The boy looked slender and weak compared to the heavy-muscled Bull. Yet Joe was well made. His muscles were long, well knit, rippling. His skin was tanned a deep brown. He had stroked his college crew and days on the river in a racing shell had covered his body with a healthy tan. His was a faster, more coordinate development. A boxer's build. Bull Mitchell was the thick-necked, more sluggish frame of a wrestler.

"Are you afraid to stand up and fight fairly, Mitchell, or will it be dirty? Fight me fair and I'll whip you."

"Make yore own rules, kid. Fair she is, and I'll bust that sweet mug of yours all over the back of yore head. Ready?" He squared off, a wide grin on his mouth. Joe was hitching up his belt. Bull leaped forward, swinging with all his weight behind that knotted fist. Joe, still with his hands at his belt, leaped lightly aside and as Bull lurched by, Joe tripped him neatly.

"Sweet," chuckled the voice of Pete Smyth who had somehow appeared, pad and pencil in hand. Beside Pete stood Kit Kavanaugh.

Bull was on his feet like a huge thing of rubber. He whirled, rushed again, missed a wild left swing. Joe's hands were up now. His right, swift, traveling but a scant twelve inches, caught Bull on the button. Joe slid from a clinch and landed a glancing blow that opened Bull's lips.

Bull, still too crazy from booze and anger to use caution, rushed again and twice more. Joe met each of those blind rushes with swift footwork and punishing jabs. Bull's mouth was bleeding. He spat, the grin gone from his battered mouth now. He was sobering up, his brain clearing, and he circled slowly, his squinting eyes watching for an opening. Joe kept just out of reach, crouched, jaw protected behind a brown shoulder, his legs moving without effort.

"Fight, you whelp," snarled Bull. "This ain't a foot race. Come on, ya yellow pup."

"Better save your wind, Mitchell." Joe shuffled forward, flat-footed, feinted, ripped a quick, punishing right to Bull's heart, and slid under the big man's swinging arm. He jerked a short one into Bull's kidneys as their bodies brushed. Bull whirled, crouched, came in with his fists jabbing. An uppercut under Joe's ribs sent the boy back. Bull's hitting power was terrific. That blow hurt. Joe covered as Bull swept him in to a clinch. The big man's gorilla arms were crushing him. Joe got one arm free and hammered on Bull's kidneys. There was no referee, no time out for rounds, no exacting rules about hitting in clinches or breaking clean. Bull's unshaven jaw was boring against Joe's shoulder.

The big man's head suddenly jerked upward against Joe's chin. Joe slid sideways and free, smashing a jab into Bull's midriff. Bull grunted and plowed after the boy. He tried to butt and Joe straightened him with an uppercut. They clinched again and this time Joe tripped and fell, the big man on top of him. Bull tried to bite Joe's ear. Joe fought in vain to slide out from under that heavy, sweating body, that crushed him into the ground.

"Fight fair, you big bum!" called Kit. "Make him quit it, somebody. This was to be a fair scrap."

"Shut up, sister," snapped Casey, on the opposite side of the clearing.

"Go button your mouth, big boy," she came back at him.

"Give him the old knee, Joe!" advised Pete Smyth.

"Bull's got 'im!" grinned Bill Clanton. "Kill 'im, Bull!"

Something happened too quickly for even Bull to know what it was. Joe was free and on his feet. The boy's face was set, terrible looking.

"Get up and fight, Mitchell!" His voice was like the snarl of a fighting dog. "Come and get it, you skunk."

Bull, a little bewildered, leaped up. He came at Joe. Joe, legs planted wide, opened his hands. His arms moved swiftly, found what they were after, and Bull Mitchell went across the boy's shoulders, somersaulting, landing with a thud on his back in the dirt.

"As neat a flying mare as ever I saw," muttered Pete Smyth, his pencil jotting down notes in shorthand. "The kid's clever, Kit."

"You gargled a mouthful, Pete. Clever—and game." She waved a roll of yellow-backed banknotes.

"Five hundred on Joe Morgan. Who wants it?"

"Make it worth while, you red-headed little cat!" Black Diamond sneered.

"Anything you say."

"Five thousand on Bull."

"Covered, dearie."

"Ain't you going a little strong, Kit?" whispered Pete Smyth.

"I'm sunk if I lose, Pete. But Joe Morgan's the only man I ever looked at twice."

Pete Smyth looked at her obliquely, his lips pursed in a soundless whistle. "Well, I'll be hanged," he grunted. "Felicitations, Kitten."

"Shut up, Pete. You're covering a fight. Tend to your knitting. Uh! Gee, Joe took that one on the chin. Why don't he pedal, Pete? He can't trade punches with that moose. Tell him, Pete."

Joe was fighting now. A terrier fighting a mastiff. Taking and giving. Kit Kavanaugh, fists clenched, was crying but did not know it.

"Joe! Joe! Joe, boy! Pedal, boy, pedal! Oh, God, Pete, he's down! That big devil's going to give him the boots."

But even as Bull Mitchell, crazy, killing mad now, leaped to jump on the face of the fallen boy was was trying to lift his numb weight off the ground, a noose sped out, tightened around Bull's shoulders, and jerked the big man backward.

Nobody had seen a man on horseback ride up. Too intent on the fight, they had not noticed him as he undid his rope and built a loop. He sat in his saddle now, a smile on his lipless mouth, Bull Mitchell on the end of his rope.

Bill Clanton jerked his gun. His shot drilled the low pulled Stetson on the rider's head. Then the man on horseback fired. Bill Clanton went down in a lump, cursing hoarsely. The rider's voice, flat and hard and menacing, cut through the tense silence.

"I'll kill any man that feels lucky. Get up and fight, kid." He slacked the rope and Bull Mitchell jerked free of its tight embrace.

"It's Wade Morgan," the sinister name of the outlaw traveled across the crowd. Almanac Jones chuckled. He stood beside Wade's horse, his white-handled gun ready. Bill Clanton sat on the ground, swaying a little, blood streaming from a smashed shoulder. From the shadows came three other riders. They lined up alongside Wade Morgan. Their drawn guns glittered in the lantern light.

Joe Morgan was on his feet now, his eyes fixed on his father who had put up his gun and was deftly coiling up the rope that had saved Joe's face from a horrible mangling. Bull Mitchell stood like a man in a trance.

"Sweet essence of sauerkraut," muttered Pete Smyth, his pencil flying, "what a break for the *Assay*, Kitten."

But Kit Kavanaugh did not hear. She was staring at Wade Morgan—Wade, white-haired, his sunken cheeks burned black by sun and wind, his eyes glittering like slits of fire in the shadow of his hatbrim. Her gaze swung to Joe. Joe, who stood there, blood-spattered, breathing hard, a terrible smile on his bleeding mouth.

"Go in and whip him, Joe!" Wade's smile was the same grim expression that widened the lips of his son. Joe nodded and faced Bull Mitchell.

"Come on, Mitchell. Nothing barred from now on. Anything goes. Come and get it. Don't anybody horn in, no matter what happens."

"Nobody'll cut in," rasped Wade Morgan. "Best man wins. Luck to you, Joe. Now fight!"

They fought. Smashing, tearing, without a rule to govern them. And those that looked on saw Bull Mitchell beaten down again and again. Saw Joe Morgan, breathing easier now that he had his second wind, stand back and let Bull Mitchell get to his feet, only to be rocked off balance again by terrible, punishing fists that crashed like sledge-hammers into the swollen, blood-smeared face of the boss of Pay Dirt.

Kit Kavanaugh, white as chalk, stared with eyes that were dark with emotion. She no longer cried or called encouragement to Joe. She seemed to be hypnotized by the bloody brutality of it all. Pete Smyth knew nothing beyond the fight and his pencil. He muttered to himself as he wrote.

While over inside the schoolhouse, behind locked doors, the fiddles and accordion played on. The caller cried himself hoarse. Women danced, peacefully unaware of what was happening out of sight and hearing of the schoolhouse. Doc Steele kept the ball rolling and the other men aided him in the deception. Amy Steele inquired about Joe.

"He's probably unable to get away from the boys, honey," Doc told her. "He'll be back before long."

Of the women there, only Hattie, mother of Joe Morgan, sensed that something was happening. She made Doc tell her. Save for the barely noticeable fact that she seemed a trifle quiet, she gave no sign of knowing that, somewhere beyond the dance, her son was fighting Bull Mitchell. Such was the fortitude of Hattie Burch.

Amy, dancing with other men, tried to hide the ache in her heart as she watched for Joe's return. Supposing he came in drunk? Or perhaps not at all? What if he chose the companionship of tipsy cowboys to her dances? She felt hurt and humiliated and more than a little angry in a pouting, ladylike way. Her father understood and teased her, trying to coax back the laughter to her lips, but his efforts were not very fruitful. The ache in the girl's heart became more poignant. At the first opportunity she slipped out an open window.

Blurred sounds of the combat came to her. She ran as fast as she could. Suddenly she came upon the ugly scene.

She saw Joe Morgan, bloody, half naked, beaten almost beyond recognition, lifting a sodden, cursing, blood-smeared man to his feet. There Bull Mitchell stood, one eye closed, his face a beaten pulp, his huge arms trying to lift the bruised, red fists that were like heavy weights. Joe Morgan braced himself on unsteady legs. Both his eyes were almost closed so that he peered, head thrust forward, like a blind man. His right arm came back slowly, fist cocked, ready to strike that final blow.

Amy Steele, with a thin cry of horror, fainted. Joe's fist crashed against Bull Mitchell's jaw. Bull dropped like a lump of dead flesh. Joe staggered, tripped, and fell across the beaten man. He tried to lift himself, then slumped forward and lay still.

Kit Kavanaugh had seen Amy Steele fall. Her lips curled a little in a smile that was half pity, half scorn. Then the gambler's daughter pushed through the crowd and knelt by Joe. Her tiny handkerchief was wiping the blood from the boy's eyes and mouth. Pete came up with a pail of water. Joe's head was in Kit's lap, his blood ruining the expensive green frock. The red-haired girl looked up, her gray eyes finding Black Diamond's hate-seared black ones.

"I'll be around in the morning to collect, dearie. And don't try any welching. I want cash. Five grand. Better take that dehorned bull home and patch him up. . . . More water, Pete."

Joe's eyes were trying to open. His heard stirred feebly. One of his battered hands tightened about Kit's, smearing it with watery blood.

"Gee, Amy, it's great of you. But you'd better go. This is . . . is no place . . . for a sweet kid like you." He went limp again. Kit's face twitched a little as if with pain. Long Bob and Pete Smyth came up. They lifted Joe to his feet and carried him down the street to his new office. Some one had taken Amy Steele back to the dance. The crowd was breaking up. For a moment Kit Kavanaugh stood there, her eyes blinking hard. Then she turned and walked away.

"Excuse me, ma'am." Kit halted, staring up at Wade Morgan who sat sideways in his saddle, his lean frame slouching gracefully. His hat was off. The light fell on his snowy hair and across his lean face.

"I don't know who you are, miss," said Wade in that flat-toned voice of his, "but whoever you are, yo're a real woman and you think a heap of that boy of mine. So do I lady. I'm proud of him. Take good care of the kid. He's worth it. . . . I wonder, if I'd write you, now and then, if I could trust you to keep quiet?"

"Do I look like a squealer, Wade Morgan?" The smile came back to Kit's face. Her gray eyes laughed at him through unshed tears. "I'll let you know how he's making it. That's what you want to ask me, wasn't it? And nobody but God and us two will ever know. Here's my hand on it."

"That makes us pardners." The bitterness was gone from Wade Morgan's face. "You're sure a real thoroughbred, ma'am. And you won't mind my tellin' you that yo're the best-lookin' girl I ever laid eyes on. That dress is plumb spoilt. Here, buy a new one with this." He pulled a roll of bills from his vest pocket. Kit laughed and shook her copper-hued head.

"Black Diamond is paying for a new one with Bull Michell's money. I won five thousand on that fight. And thanks for roping Bull Mitchell. You saved me the trouble of shooting him. And I never shot a man in my life."

"You mean that—"

"That my finger was on the trigger when you jerked the Bull over backwards. You see, I think a lot of Joe. I don't want a man with a smashed-in face."

"Yo're Joe's best girl?"

"No. He's my best, my one and only man. There's a difference. Joe still calls me Miss Kavanaugh. He never saw me till today. It's all on my side. If you can waste half an hour, come over to my cabin and I'll tell you the terrible details about how I'm laying for your son. You can then wish me luck or tell me I'm a damn fool or both."

"Sorry, ma'am, but I can't take yuh up on that invite. Some friends of mine are a-waitin' for me. We're in a hurry. And I'm wishin' you that luck you want."

She gripped his hand in both of hers. "Write to Kit Kavanaugh. Sign it Amigo and I'll know. I'd know anyhow, because I haven't had a letter from anybody in years. Good luck, Wade Morgan. I'll take care of Joe."

The dance was breaking up. The folks were calling "Good night, everybody," as they scattered. Kit passed the closed door of Joe Morgan's office. Voices came from inside. Hattie and Mrs. Steele were standing outside consoling Amy who looked ill and was sobbing softly. Kit, keeping to the shadows, halted at the rear door of Pete Smyth's newspaper office. A light burned inside the drawn shades. Kit opened the door and went in. Pete sat on the floor among the litter of paper and type cases and bulk paper. He was pounding away on a battered typewriter. Almanac Jones sat on a packing box, a bottle of whisky beside him, brows knitted, a stubby pencil scribbling words on a thick yellow pad. They were getting out the first edition of the Pay Dirt *Assay*.

Kit laid a hand on Pete's shoulder. "Remember, Pete," she said, "you two comic valentines are due at my shack for breakfast at eight o'clock sharp. Promise, or I'll refuse to read your darn paper."

Pete nodded, looked up and grinned. "Almanac, old kid, set the alarm clock for eight o'clock. Otherwise we'll be too busy to note the time."

"Who gits shot at eight?" inquired Almanac, reaching for the clock.

"Nobody," said Kit sternly, "gets even half-shot. Do you like waffles, Almanac?"

"Yes'm."

"Then follow Pete when that alarm goes off. Good night, boys." Kit Kavanaugh went home to her empty cabin. When she had undressed and put out the light, she stood by the darkened window, looking up at the stars.

"God, I've never asked You for much. I've always been able to rustle and others needed Your help more than I did. But to-night I'm asking You to give me Joe Morgan. I know I'm no lady like the little Amy kid, but I've kept myself clean as I could. I'll take care of him, God. I'll help him. I'll never quit

him or cheat on him. If he goes bad like his father went bad,
I'll go along with him. I'll stick to him, win, lose, or draw.
Amen."

Chapter Ten

KIT PLAYS HER HAND

DOC STEELE patched up Joe Morgan, then tended to Bull
Mitchell and Bill Clanton. Bull, over in Black Diamond's cabin,
lay in sullen silence while the genial Doc tended him. Black Diamond
paced the floor like a tigress. Doc then went to the saloon
to fix up Bill Clanton.

Bill Clanton was more scared than hurt. The bullet had ripped
away the flesh but had not broken any bones. He slobbered and
whined and yelled whenever Doc touched the wound.

"Gawd, the old lady'll kill me when I git home. She'll skin
me alive. Gawdamight, I'm a pore, sufferin' critter. Ouch! I'm
sufferin' horrible. Gimme a bottle, Casey."

Casey gave him a bottle and took his pay from the wounded
man's greasy overalls.

"No more free drinks, ya lousy bum. How's young Morgan
look, Doc? Bull kin fire me fer sayin' so, but 'at kid's a champ.
A champ, no less."

Doc Steele grinned and nodded.

"He put himself through college, Casey, with his fists. Fought
under another name. Only one man between him and the middle-
weight crown right now and men like John L., Corbett, and
Jeffries claim he's a cinch."

The eyes under Casey's battered brows lit up with admiration.

"Wot a cleanin' he took Bull to. No wonder. Tell the kid I'm
for him, Doc. Bull's a good guy in some ways, when ya know
'im. Mebby he'll shake wit' the kid and call it a day. Bull's mean
when he's drunk, but he's game, Doc, he's game."

Doc took the women home. Long Bob met them down the
road. He had ridden a way with Wade and his companions of
the night. Alamanac had been instructed by Bob to look after
Joe. Joe, battered and lame all over, had been put to bed and
told to stay there. His mother had come in and tucked him
in as if he were a small boy.

"Of course, I'm not mad at you, Joe. I'm proud of you. We're
all mighty proud of you."

"Has Amy gone home?" he had asked.

"Yes."

It was a mother's lie. The sort of lie that is more blessed than truth. And somehow Joe Morgan knew she lied and loved her all the more for it. Hattie was a real pardner. The boy smiled gamely and dropped off into a weary slumber filled with chaotic dreams. Through those dreams danced a red-haired girl in a dull green frock—the prettiest girl Joe had ever known. A girl of the dance halls and bar-rooms, a female gambler . . . but beautiful as a goddess.

At eight in the morning someone shook Joe's shoulder. His swollen, blackened eyes looked up into two faces.

"Git up, Little Britches. Us men has got tuh rattle our hocks. We're goin' tuh breakfast. Ain't we, Pete?"

"A real breakfast, brother Morgan. Cream waffles, honey, fresh fruit, coffee with whiskers. Up, up, Josephus, the sun has riz. Can you see with those orchid hued orbs? Then feast your orbs upon this first copy of the first edition of the snappiest little sheet that ever came off a press. It's a bearcat though I say it myself. Pithy with news. A sporting page, a society column, range topics by my able assistant, Almanac Jones, the world's greatest columnist. He adds a dash of poetry. Personal interview with the notorious Wade Morgan. An editorial that will knock the populace for a goal. If this paper ain't a dinger, I'll take my type and swallow it whole. Come on, Joe, we're partaking of a morning banquet with our marvelous society editor."

Kit, in a simple little house dress, met them at her door with a smile that was more than cordial. If two of her morning guests were somewhat intoxicated and the other was a battered wreck, she gave no sign of knowing it. She placed them at a table that boasted real Irish linen, sterling silver, real china and delicate glassware. Never had three men sat down to a more enticing breakfast. Beside each plate lay a folded copy of the Pay Dirt *Assay*.

So began Joe Morgan's first morning as the only attorney in Pay Dirt. A memorable one. Kit Kavanaugh mothered them and bullied them and made them laugh. . . .

"And if you boys can stand my cooking, I'll turn this into a private boarding-house. You can't be eating that greasy truck the Chinaman throws across his counter. All three of you need a woman to boss you around."

Pete Smyth rose solemnly.

"Boys, I've known Kit Kavanaugh since she wore her hair in

funny little pigtails and had freckles bigger than half dollars. Her father and I were pals. Before she was ten years old, she bossed us. I could tell you tales, gentlemen, of those good old days in New York, in San Francisco, in Denver, in Chicago where our trails crossed. Tales that will make you laugh and cry. Boys, stand up and drink, in cold, sparkling water, a toast. I give you, in a spirit of love, respect, and profound admiration Kathleen Mavourneen Kavanaugh, the most wonderful little girl on earth."

They drank standing. Kit's lips trembled a little when she thanked Pete Smyth with misty eyes.

When her three guests had gone, Kit Kavanaugh slipped a small pearl-handled pistol into her jacket pocket and walked down to Bull Mitchell's saloon to collect the bet she had won from Black Diamond. Joe Morgan, from his office, saw her boldly enter the front door. He felt strangely upset and annoyed and fought back the urge to cross the street and make her come away. Then he saw her emerge, smiling, a roll of bills in her hands. She looked like a boy in her tailored riding breeches, hiking boots, and buckskin jacket decorated with gay-colored porcupine quills. A man's soft felt hat hid her copper-colored hair. She walked with an athletic, boyish stride.

Behind her, in the doorway, stood Casey and Bull Mitchell, the latter leaning on a cane, his face swathed in snowy bandages. But behind those bandages was a face distorted with black anger. True to his gambler's code, Bull had paid Black Diamond's lost wager.

Perhaps it was not entirely the loss of the money that angered the big saloon-keeper. He saw her swing into Joe Morgan's office. With a muttered curse he limped back inside and told Casey to mix up a drink composed of absinthe and rye whisky. Casey's grin vanished when Bull's bloodshot, slitted eyes glared at him from under puffed, blackened lids.

Kit walked into Joe Morgan's office.

"Five grand, Joe. Won it on the fight. A new frock, a bottle of terribly expensive and silly perfume, and a good saddle horse for yours truly. A swell-elegant desk and files for the Attorney-at-Law, sometimes known as Little Britches, in certain pugilistic circles as the Bronco Kid. . . . The secret's out, Casey slipped it to me. A decent cot and bedroom things for Peter Bartholomew Smyth, Y as in wine. Store clothes, checked preferred, with a red and green vest, for Almanac Jones, columnist of the Pay Dirt Assay. The rest goes to charity. Thus the raging Bull becomes a philanthropist in disguise. Quit scowling, Joe, you'll open that cut over your eye."

Joe tried to grin. A man on horseback came up the street. The rider was Sim Patchen and his horse was dripping with sweat. He swung to the ground and burst into the office of Peg Leg, Justice of the Peace. His loud bellow carried up and down and across the dusty street.

"Git a posse together. Hell's tuh pay! Sheriff from Miles City's at the Clanton place. Wade Morgan and three others stuck up the train and got off with fifty thousand! They come this way! Git a posse!"

Men poured from the saloons as the news spread. Sim Patchen was shouting orders. Peg Leg was hobbling about like a man gone crazy. Horses were being saddled. Guns bristled. Bull Mitchell was already mounted, armed, bandaged, impatient to be off.

"Steady, boy," said Kit Kavanaugh, gripping Joe's arm in a tight pressure. "Steady's the word. Let 'em yell and cuss and bluster and ride away in a dust cloud. They'll come back with a headache and without any prisoners. Keep your shirt on, boy."

"He stood by me last night," muttered Joe, pawing in an opened kit-bag and dragging out a cartridge belt and holstered gun. "He's my Dad. They're going after him. It's up to me to—"

"To sit tight and wait for some cash customers." Kit took the belt and gun. "Think Wade Morgan would want you messing up in this? Be sane, pardner."

There were times when Kit was more man than she was woman— Steady-nerved, cool-brained, sensible. Women such as she had, in other times, steadied toppling thrones and ruled empires. She gently pushed Joe into a chair and held him there, her hands on his shoulders. The posse rode away at a gallop, Bull Mitchell and Sim Patchen leading them.

"Now," she said, "let's drop in at the office of the Pay Dirt *Assay*. I thought I heard a lovely snoring duet there as I passed. Bet you a dime to ten dollars that our up and doing journalists have slept through the excitement and missed a big scoop. A favorable symptom. Last night's work tired 'em out.

"I've seen Pete Smyth come out of one of those terrible benders seeing pink elephants ridden by gnomes with purple ears and green whiskers. One of the greatest men in the game, Pete Smyth. He's covered some of the biggest assignments in newspaper history. Wounded twice in the Boer War, once in Cuba. He's poked into China's forbidden cities, crashed the gates of a Turkish harem, was held by natives in the interior of South America. Shot his way out and his series of stories on that Aztec city of gold is a classic, even if Pete never saw such a place except in his dreams.

"He's a genius—and a famous drunkard. Booze is his disease, poor devil. Perhaps, if we can hold him here in Pay Dirt and keep him sober part of the time, he'll be happy. I'd do anything for Pete. He'd never admit it, but he's done a lot to keep Kit Kavanaugh from going to hell. He's bought books for me to read and made me read 'em. Good books. He's the only school I ever went to. Dad was clever, but no man could ever mistake him for a scholar. Pete always stayed with us when we met him in our travels. He and Dad used to get on some of the darndest sprees you ever saw. Always they brought home some sort of peace offering. Once it was a trick gander, another time it was a round trip ticket to Paris. A one-horse hack, a baby elephant, a Chinese idol that almost got us all into a tong war, a truckload of imported gowns, flowers, candy by the crate, Jew's-harps, pianos, three Negro maids at one crack, a monkey, hand-organ and wop thrown in. Spanish shawls, wooden shoes, kippered herrings done up with red ribbons, and other such gifts.

"Who couldn't forgive 'em? I'd put them both to bed and nurse 'em through the jim-jams. Listen to their promises just as if I believed them. And then do it all over again. When an editor had lost Pete and couldn't find him in jail, he'd send over a messenger to our house with Pete's pay-check and walking papers. That's why I'll always think an awful lot of Pete. It's folks you do things for, Joe, that you love the most."

Joe Morgan nodded. He was looking at the picture of Amy Steele, there on his second-hand desk in its silver frame. Amy had done a lot for Joe, in her child's way. Trivial, girlish little things to be sure, yet the young lawyer knew that those small gestures had been prompted by a certain affection for him. Yet, last night, when he really needed her, she had not come. Joe knew now that it was this strange, very beautiful red-haired girl who had held his battered head in her lap and sponged away the blood. He was beginning to remember, now. Who was Kit Kavanaugh? Or rather, what was she? Nice girls didn't go boldly into saloons in broad daylight to collect bets on fights. They didn't nurse men like Pete Smyth through periods of delirium tremens. They didn't have men to breakfast.

As if the girl read his thoughts, she smiled and deftly rolled a cigarette. Her gray eyes were bright with dancing, teasing laughter.

"May I have a match, please?" she asked, her voice, throaty and rich in tone, had the same hint of gay mockery as her eyes. Joe knew she was baiting him and he squirmed uncomfortably as he lit her cigarette. Smoking among women, save certain kinds of women, had not yet invaded the cow country.

"Does it make you uncomfortable, Joe, to have a notorious woman in breeches sitting on the corner of your desk smoking? Of course it does," she answered her own question. "Did you know that I made my living gambling? Did you, Joe?"

"No," replied Joe, annoyance in his tone, "I didn't. And if I did, it wouldn't make any difference."

"Any difference in what?" she asked, her red mouth, a tiny bit too large for a girl's mouth, quirking at the corners.

"In anything. I mean I don't go around picking my friends to pieces hunting their faults like a monkey hunting fleas. It don't matter what you do for a living."

"That's boy's talk, Joe. Of course, it makes a difference. Supposing I were one of Black Diamond's percentage girls? You wouldn't want me here, in plain view of the passersby, perched on your desk trying to blow smoke rings. You know, Joe, I've batted around this queer old world since I was knee high to a burro. I've seen men of all kinds—from thugs and hop-heads to bankers and railroad presidents. Most of them had a rotten streak in 'em.

"They'll get a few drinks, even those sedate and dignified bankers, and act like idiots over some frail with peroxide hair and baby blue eyes and a lisp that's as easily wiped off as the rouge on their lips. But let them be driving along the street when this same girl comes along. Your banker will carefully look the opposite direction. The world knows what she is, anyhow, as she comes down the main stem on her high heels, in her silk and fur. She's at least no hypocrite. But your banker don't dare reveal his real self except behind locked doors in a dim light.

"No, Joe boy, you wouldn't want me here if I were a bad woman. That's the term they use—'bad women.' And if my conscience weren't clean, I wouldn't be here. And if Amy Steele came along, you wouldn't be embarrassed."

She hadn't meant to let slip that last sentence.

"Supposing we leave Amy Steele's name out." Joe's voice was sharp.

"My mistake. I humbly apologize. Well, see you in jail, Joe." Kit Kavanaugh swung from her perch on the shabby desk and went out whistling, her hands in the pockers of her breeches. Spots of bright red stained her cheeks. "Darn, darn, darn . . . damn!"

She climbed the steep slope of the mountain to a spot almost at its top. There, on a broad, flat rock, she lay, her head pillowed in her arms, and her slim body shook with sobs.

Chapter Eleven

TRAPPED

FOR almost half an hour Kit lay there. Her sobbing ceased. She may have been asleep. Then a throaty little laugh came from her hidden mouth. She sat up, not a trace of grief left in her eyes. From the pockets of her buckskin jacket she took some stale biscuits and few some saucy little tree squirrels that did not see to fear her. A magpie joined the feast, hopping about brazenly, scolding.

To this spot that overlooked countless of miles of rolling hills and prairie, the girl was wont to bring her troubles. Here among the pines, lost from the clatter of the mill and the sordid noises of the camp, she came, as a pilgrim goes to a shrine. Pine needles and wild roses. Tiny crimson dots that were wild strawberries. Mountain wild flowers decorating this stone altar unmarred by man's profane handling.

Kit called the big stone slab her Wishing Stone. Because the beautiful whimsical romance of Ireland filled her heart, she sat there, when the weather favored, and dreamed all sorts of things. And while she had never made a wish there, she promised herself with the utmost faith in its fulfillment, that she would some day sit there and make a wish and that wish would be fulfilled.

From a russet leather case, Kit took a pair of small but powerful binoculars. She liked to sit there and sweep those hills with the glasses. Sometimes the glasses found nothing but grazing cattle and horses. Now and then a lone rider or two. Perhaps a team pulling a buggy or buckboard or wagon to town. A freight outfit, creeping along the yellow ribbon of road. A round-up outfit at work, its white tents spotting some creek or water hole, it riders swinging in from circle with their drives. Indian camps and breed camps.

For half an hour Kit's glasses swung here and there. She was watching Sim Patchen's posses combing the hills and coulées in their fruitless hunt for Wade Morgan—Wade, who would most likely be across the Missouri River by now, heading for the Hole-in-the-Wall country. Patchen's men and the Miles City posse were heading for the badlands. Fanshaped, they rode on, slipping out of sight in long draws and deep coulées, reappearing again.

The glasses paused at the Morgan-Burch ranch. No sign of life there. Long Bob was with the round-up, camped around the shoulder of Two Buttes, working the Sagebrush Flats country below the Circle C.

The glasses moved on. Past Bull Mitchell's, past the schoolhouse, on to Steele's place. A lone rider was leaving Doc Steele's ranch below the school section—a rider forking a white horse. Even at a distance Kit recognized the white singlefooter, the silver-mounted bridle and saddle that caught and reflected the morning sunlight. Amy Steele. The milkwhite gelding was a present from Joe Morgan. Kit knew that, even as every one in that part of the country knew it. In the cow country, when a man gives a girl a valuable horse like that five-gaited white gelding that Joe had broken, gentled, and given Amy Steele, cow-country gossip has it that the gift is in the nature of a betrothal gift.

Amy rode slowly along the winding road that led to Pay Dirt.

"She's thought it over, listened to Doc, and is coming to town to square herself. The pot congeals. Your move, Kitten. Don't hit below the belt, dearie. Oh, darn, let the kid come. Give her a break, Kit. That's the gal, big-hearted Kit Kavanaugh. But look out, little prairie flower. If you get too dangerous, mother will have to use a marked deck. Sorry, kid, but he's my man and what I want, I fight for to hold."

Idly her glasses followed the girl on the white horse. Then Kit noticed two other riders that left the Clanton ranch. They also headed for town, traveling at a long trot.

"The Clanton whelps, coming to town after their old man. And what Bill Clanton's old woman will do to him will be more than plenty.   Hmmm. They're in a hurry No doubt they've spotted the maiden on the white horse and have a double case of calf-love. Quite so. In the spring, a young man's fancy
Poor kid, she'll have to listen to the drunken bragging of that unwashed pair of deuces. I wouldn't inflict those two brutes on my worst enemy There's your rose between two thorns. Poor kid."

Kit put aside the glasses and threw more biscuit crumbs to the very persistent and indignant magpie that hopped about her almost within arm's reach.

"All right, Foxy Quiller. Here's the last handout. Now beat it." Kit stretched out lazily on her back and watched some fleecy white clouds make pictures against the azure sky Not a sound marred the silence of the mountainside. Half an hour later she sat up, yawned luxuriously with outstretched arms.

"Better get down and rustle grub for my boarders." She started to put away the glasses, then changed her mind. She lifted them to her eyes. A sharp exclamation broke from her.

For down there, at the edge of the rough gullies that joined the mountains to the rolling hills, a drama was being enacted. Amy Steele and her white horse were racing for home. Behind her tore the two Clantons, quirting and spurring. The white horse was gaining, out-distancing the two men.

Then Kit saw the white horse falter, go down, flop over. A badger hole, perhaps. The white gelding scrambled to its feet and trotted off a way, then stood still, halted by the draging bridle reins, no doubt. But Amy Steele did not move. The Clantons loped up, jerked to a halt, were off their horses, just as Amy Steele gained her feet. There was a brief struggle.

One of the Clantons fetched back the white horse. Amy was lifted to the saddle. Again they came on toward town, the white horse in the middle as they rode three abreast. Half a mile. Then the three riders quit the main road and were lost to sight in a long, brush-matted draw.

And though Kit Kavanaugh watched for more than an hour, none of the three riders again appeared.

"Well, it's none of my business."

Kit put away her binoculars and made her way back down the mountainside.

Chapter Twelve

NICK OF TIME

ALMANAC Jones and Pete Smyth were at Tex Buford's place. Kit sent a miner down there to tell them to "come and get it." She had passed Joe's office. His door was open. He sat at his desk, bent over an open law book. Kit knew that he had seen her when she went into the *Assay* office. He was deliberately ignoring her. She wanted to go in and muss up his hair and tell him to quit pouting. But a sreak of stubborn pride forbade that when she noticed a cold lunch and a bottle of beer beside the big law books.

Kit greeted Almanac and Pete. She set out a bottle and two glasses.

"You need about one more stiff jolt before you tackle this feed. Gosh, what a fine pair of hangovers. When you've wrapped yourselves around this grub pile, go out and buy a shave apiece."

They exchanged sheepish glances. Kit poured their drinks. When Pete had downed his, he looked at her.

"Let's have it, Kitten. Both barrels. We're a pair of soaks. Fire when you're ready, Gridley."

"We'll omit the browbeating, this time, Pete."

"You ain't sick or anything, Kitten?"

"Nope. But I'm doing something mean, Pete, and my conscience is riding me. Now wade into that soup before it gets cold. Then you get some milk toast."

"We stopped for Joe," said Pete, watching her closely. "He said he'd had lunch."

Kit nodded. "Yes." She turned to Almanac. "Another shot of that hooch will fix you. Hair of the dog bit you."

"Doggone, yuh shore savvy what a man needs, ma'am."

Between sips of the hot soup, Pete kept watching the girl. He knew that something was troubling her and that the something had to do with Joe Morgan. She stood by the window, staring with troubled eyes at nothing, her hands deep in her pockets. Suddenly she turned.

"Could I borrow your horse for the afternoon, Almanac?"

"Shore thing. Mind how yuh git on him, fer he don't stand good. Outside uh that, he's plumb gentle."

"I'll manage." Kit took a light carbine from her gun rack as she went out. "Pile the dishes in the sink, boys," she called back over her shoulder.

Some minutes later Kit Kavanaugh rode out of town. Once beyond the bend in the road she gave the big sorrel his head and reined him off the main road along a narrow trail.

An hour later she was riding up the wooded draw into which Amy Steele and the two Clantons has vanished. An old wood road led up the draw. She dismounted and slid the carbine from the saddle scabbard. Now she went on afoot. In a small clearing stood a deserted log cabin. Nearby three saddle horses grazed, reins trailing. One of the horses was Amy Steel's white gelding. The sweat-marked bay and black wore the Clanton iron. The cabin door was shut. Muffled voices came from inside. Kit ran lightly toward the cabin, approaching it from one end that had no window.

"Lay a paw on her again, Tug, and by Gawd, I'll blow yore dang head off. Maw said as I was the one that cud have 'er."

"That's a damn lie! Git back from me, Tim. Put down that gun. Amy said she liked me better. She's a-gonna marry me or nobody!"

Kit peered through broken space in the chinking. Amy Steele, her face white and tear-stained, crouched back against the wall, her eyes wide with stark terror. The two Clantons stood in the center of the dirt floor. There was a six-shooter in Tim's hand. Tug's fists were doubled.

"Dad and Joe Morgan will kill you two for this!" Amy's voice was husky with fear.

They paid no heed. Both of them were insanely drunk.

"They'll lynch you both!" shrilled the girl.

"Fer what? We ain't hurtin' yuh. Don't aim tuh hurt yuh." This from Tim who seemed less drunk than his brother. "Ain't I bin tellin' Tug not tuh tetch yuh? Ain't I? I'm a white man, I am. I got stock in my own iron an' Bull Mitchell 'lowed he'd gimme plenty more on shares an' lemme run his place. I got sense. Dang it, I'm good enough fer any woman, I am. Git back, Tug, er I'll gut-shoot yuh!"

He cocked the .45. Tug backed away, his face mottled with cowardly fear. Tim's gun swung slowly upward. His eyes were red with murder.

"I'm gonna kill yuh. Fer if I don't, yuh'll kill me. She cain't belong tuh two of us."

Tim backed away a step, crouching, his face working horribly.

The deafening roar of a gun. Amy Steele screamed. But Tug Clanton did not fall. Tim stood there, his jaw hanging loosely, staring with stupid, horrified eyes at his right hand that was bleeding. His Colt .45 lay unfired on the dirt floor.

"Now, you two mangy coyotes," came Kit Kavanaugh's tense voice from a paneless window, "get your horses and hit the grit. Ride hard, because there'll be some men right behind you. When they catch up, there'll be a necktie party. This country's too clean for such dirty skunks as you two. Now rattle your dew claws, coyotes. If this gun goes off again, there'll be a double funeral in the Clanton tribe."

The two Clantons lost no time in getting away. When they had gone, Kit went inside and put an arm about Amy's quivering shoulders.

"Have a good cry, honey, then you'll feel better. Then we'll ride on back to your ranch. And nobody will ever know what's happened here. I've thrown a scare into those two toughs that will keep them traveling in a high lope till they cross the Canadian line or the Mexican border. And we'll just say nothing and nobody'll ever know. Did . . . did I get here soon enough?"

"Soon enough? I don't understand."

"What I mean is, child, did anything . . . happen?"

"Oh!" Amy's face went crimson, then white as death. "No. Thank God, thank God . . . and I'll never forget what you've done, never, so long as I live. If only some day I can do something, anything, to—"

"Whoa, honey. Don't. Don't promise a thing. Promises are like a light pack. Easy to carry the first few miles, then they get heavy. A promise is a debt and debts are burdens. Just call it a day. And don't go out riding alone like that unless you pack a gat or at least brass knuckles or a black-jack or a nice sharp knife. You can't be too careful, these days, about the men you play around with. Feeling better? Then let's go bye-bye. I have to get back to my cabin. Company for supper. You know what that means. Men never realize what fuss a woman goes to when she sets out a decent meal. And wait till I pin up your clothes. Hmmm. Black and blue marks on your arms and shoulders. Tell the folks your horse fell. That's no lie. I saw him go tail over applecart. I'll help alibi you. And quit trying to thank me because it makes me feel like a bum. You see, it happens that I don't like you. Nothing personal. Just one of those things."

"You don't like me?" echoed Amy Steele. "Have I hurt you in any way?"

"Heavens, no. Let's not go into it. I really can't explain it. But I'm glad I came along. Like the Boy Scout, I've done my one good deed to-day. We're going to have a grand sunset this evening. Look at the pinkish light on Two Buttes. Don't you adore this country?"

"I'd rather live in the city. I love the crowds and lights and the gaity. Have you ever lived in the city, Miss Kavanaugh?"

"Yes," Kit smiled oddly. "New York, San Francisco, Paris, Buenos Aires, London, Monte Carlo. I've never been able to remember a real home. Only flats and apartments and hotels. Some of the best, a few of the worst. You speak of gaiety. Have you ever seen the other side of the city? The poverty and crime and filth and darkness? No, even your funny little slumming parties that show you a lot of faked tricks that make you shiver, cannot even give you the most remote idea of what lies beneath. Things that make your blood stop going. Poverty that makes you heartsick so that you can't sleep at nights. Women's tears, the pitibul, begging hands of starving children. Crimes that make plain murder look like a kindly deed. That's the city. May God let me stay out here where it's big and clean and quiet and where you soul finds rest. . . . But gee, we'd better hit a lope. Remember, now, your horse fell."

"Why, if you hate me, are you doing this for me?"

"Ask me something easy." Kit let her big sorrel hit a long lope. Amy followed behind, then caught up. She asked no more questions.

"Her horse fell," Kit told Doc Steele and his wife. "No thanks, I can't stay to supper. Have company waiting at home."

A light burned through the dusk, showing Joe Morgan sitting at his desk, a pipe between his teeth. Kit leaped from her horse and burst in without the formality of a knock.

"I'll call grub pile in just one hour. Just time for you to finish this most important law case involving untold millions. If you persist in sitting here like a hop-toad on a lily pad, I'll set fire to the joint. See the journalists?"

"They're out peddling their papers," grinned Joe. "I'm sorry I acted rude, Kit. I—"

"Put it in writing, pardner, or say it with orchids. Speaking of flowers, hot-house and wild, if you're not too far engrossed in the gigantic affairs of this business of laying the law down to the people, I'll let you come along with me, some morning or some evening, up to a certain spot on the side of the mountain. Some day when your soul seems to need a bath and massage, if you know what I'm getting at."

When she had gone, Joe Morgan still sat there, his cold pipe in his hand, the lingering ghost of a smile on his lips. His glance strayed to Amy's picture on his desk and he reddened guiltily.

Chapter Thirteen

QUARANTINE

A WHITE wolf sat on the rim of a hill and howled at the moon. A wrinkled old Sioux told Pete Smyth that it was a sign. A sign from the great Manitou. The sign of death.

That was in October. Pete wrote a little feature story and ran it in his *Assay*. Later that winter people remembered the prophecy. For with the December snows, just before the Chrismas holidays, death skulled through the drifted streets of Pay Dirt. Two miners were found dead in their shack. Others were down in bed. Doc Steele asked Pete Smyth to print some signs in red lettering. A dozen signs each bearing a large, black dread label: "Smallpox."

Fate plays no favorites. Children, burly miners, the women of Whisky Gulch. The chilled-steel miners' picks clawed out shallow graves in the frozen ground. Pete Smyth printed another dozen red signs. The mills shut down and the school was closed. Pay Dirt went into a siege of quarantine. No person was allowed to leave town. None could enter. Quarrels were forgotten, old enmities put aside as Pay Dirt banded together to fight the plague.

Kit Kavanaugh and Amy Steele were the first to volunteer as nurses. Mrs. Steele went everywhere with her husband, for the scourge had reached out its fleshless hands and scattered its curse among the ranches and the Indian and breed camps. What little sleep Doc obtained, he got between visits when Mrs. Steele drove Dobbin across the drifted hills.

Up in Whisky Gulch, Black Diamond put her silks and velvets and jewels in her trunk. When Doc Steele came on his next visit, she wore the white uniform of a trained nurse. Something of the bitterness and hardness was gone from her face.

"Bull rustled some cots, Doctor. I've turned the dance hall into a ward. I can take six more outside patients."

"Good stuff. You've had training?"

"Ten years of it, Doctor." She no longer called him "Doc."

Joe Morgan stood on the board walk in front of his office. He was waiting to take Kit to some breed camps. Across the street stood Bull Mitchell, looking like a mamoth bear in his buffalo coat and fur cap. Across the frozen street, the two enemies eyed one another. Then Joe Morgan crossed over.

"Come in and have a drink before you start," growled Bull. Joe followed the big man inside. They stood at the bar and Casey, his small eyes alight with wonder, served them.

"Here's burying the hatchet, Morgan."

"Here's to it, Bull."

"Till the quarantine is lifted, Morgan."

"Till then, Bull."

And so that deadline that divided Pay Dirt ceased, for the time, to exist.

Pete Smyth and Almanac Jones did all manner of odd jobs and errands for Kit Kavanaugh and Amy Steele. Joe Morgan helped Bull Mitchell pack mattresses and bedding to the dance-hall ward. Tex Buford closed his saloon and handled the busines of freighting in the supplies and mail from a place down the road where the freight and mail from the outside was dumped at the quarantine line.

Peg Leg Love was down with the smallpox. Sim Patchen was kept busy enforcing the quarantine. Some of the bohunk miners and cousin Jacks were ugly and wanted to escape and Sim had his hands full. No man among the less ignorant of Pay Dirt failed to do his share. Each night claimed its quota of dead. The grave-diggers were using powder now.

One day Long Bob Burch drove into town. In the bobsled, under the quilts and blankets, lay Joe's mother, her care-worn face flushed with fever. Kit Kavanaugh, standing on the side-walk, nodded understandingly before Bob could speak. "Take her to my house." Kit slid into the seat beside Long Bob.

Three nights later, Hattie smiled up at Joe and Long Bob—

a long, weary sigh—and she closed her tired eyes. Her troubles on this earth were forever gone. Kit led the two stunned, grief-stricken men into the next room, then returned to pull the white sheet across the face of Hattie. Death had softened the dead woman's face. There was a contented little smile on her lips.

Kit went back to the two men. Amy had come in, her face colored from the winter night. She sat beside Joe on the couch, her arm about his shoulders. Long Bob sat apart, his face hidden in his big hands. Kit poured Bob a stiff drink and made him swallow it.

"And now I want you and Joe to go down to the *Assay* office. Amy will go with you."

When they came back at daylight, Kit had dressed Hattie in the simple little black dress that she had worn the day she married Bob. A carpenter from the mill had made a coffin of pine boards and Kit had covered it with black cloth. In the folded, work-worn hands that looked strangely transparent now, Kit had placed a little bouquet of artificial flowers.

In the gray light of another sorrow-laden day, Hattie, mother of Joe Morgan, was buried. Pete Smyth, in a clear, low tone, read the funeral service.

What heartaches, what woman's grief had been her lot, this girl who had left home to go with Wade Morgan and become the mother of his son. . . . There, gathering dust in the gun rack at the ranch, her father's Winchester, reminder of his only visit. Kit had gotten the story from Almanac Jones. She thought of it now. Had Hattie still kept that love for Wade Morgan in her heart? Because she was a woman, because she loved the son of Wade Morgan, Kit wondered about those things as she bowed her head.

And when the funeral was over, they went back along the road to town, the sled runners creaking dismally across the frozen ground. It occurred to Kit Kavanaugh that the day was Christmas day. Her father had always made much of Christmas day. He and Kit had always been together on that day. There had always been a tree. And presents. Some years the presents were lavish, other years the bits of beribboned tissue paper held only cheap little gifts. But they had always been gay and cheerful and had made much ado about it. . . . And this was another sort of Christmas. . . . Peace on earth, good will toward men.

Kit changed into white and went up to Whisky Gulch to help Black Diamond. Bull Mitchell lay on one of the cots.

"Merry Christmas, Bull."

Kit made herself smile.

Chapter Fourteen

THE SIX-SHOOTER

AGAIN the wild roses were in bloom. Pete Smyth and Alamanac Jones labored at their printing shop. A huge pile of posters were stacked on the floor in one corner of a littered office.

JOE MORGAN
FOR
DISTRICT ATTORNEY

The printing press halted. Pete Smyth reached for his coat. "As campaign manager for brother Morgan, I hereby predict, and am willing to bet small change or yellow-backed money that our man wins by ten lengths. Shake a leg there, Almanac."

"Gawdamighty, I'm wore out shakin' 'em now. Where's them tacks. Where'd yuh put that hammer?"

"In the buckboard with the cigars and beer. Did Tex put in that jug of red-eye?"

"Two jugs. The brown 'un is fer the breed votes. T'other fer the illegal citizens. Bull Mitchell an' that danged whipsnapper candidate uh his pulled out an hour ago."

"Which, my well meaning but somewhat befuddled fellow-conspirator, is in keeping with my plan of campaign. Kid Nap had nothing on Peter Bartholomew Smyth, Y as it is used in Wile, when it comes to strategy. Being an hour in the rear of Bull Mitchell and that gyp-artist he's ballyhooing for district attorney, our idea is to simply cover their posters with ours."

"Doggone! Danged if you ain't smarter'n a bank robber, Pete. Who is this Kid Nap party yuh speak of?"

"Napoleon, none other. The one and only. Where's that bottle?"

Pay Dirt was in the throes of wild excitement. Campaign banners covered every available foot of wall space. One side of the street was solidly plastered with huge posters urging one and all to vote for Joe Morgan. While the other side of the street was unanimous in their support of Ben Thrasher, who was Bull Mitchell's protégé and candidate for the office of district attorney.

The campaign was at its height. Pay Dirt's deadline was more vividly in existence than ever before. It promised to become one of the hardest fought and bitterest political battles that section of Montana had ever witnessed.

Pete Smyth had fired the opening gun of the battle. The Pay Dirt *Assay* had come out with scarehead captions that branded Bull Mitchell as a dangerous, undesirable citizen, a menace to propriety, a lodestone hung about the neck of law and order.

BULL'S HORNS MUST BE SAWED
WHISKY GULCH MUST GO!
JOE MORGAN PROMISES PEACE

Our esteemed fellow-townsman, a native-born citizen, a man famed for his aggressive courage and fearlessness, comes out with frank statement of his views. You who would drag the fair name of Pay Dirt in the muck of infamy, read this and weep. In a special interview with Attorney Joe Morgan, he outlined to this writer his ideas, his ideals, and his platform. Those of you readers who believe in a government of equality, of justice, of right, will need to read no further. I appeal to those on the fence. I shall strive, in words that are plain to read, to pull from your eyes the black blindfold that Bull Mitchell has put there. I will prove to you that Bull Mitchell is a menace. And I will prove that Sim Patchen and Peg Leg Love accept from Bull Mitchell rewards for service. Bribes. You know what a bribe is? I give you here, its definition, then. It is something that no man can hand Joe Morgan! . . .

For the ensuing two days following the publication of that free edition of the Pay Dirt *Assay*, Pete Smyth and Almanac Jones stayed in their barricaded office. Kit brought their meals under the protection of a white flag of truce. Bill and Sim Patchen walked back and forth with sawed-off shotguns in their arms. Joe and Long Bob were away at the time, campaigning on horseback, visiting ranches and round-up camps and the small settlements of invading dry-land farmers who had begun to trickle into the open rangeland.

It was Black Diamond who conceived the idea of Bull's buying a newspaper and thus getting his views into print. Her nurse's uniform packed away, she again reigned as the queen of Whisky Gulch. Kit told Pete that if Joe should be defeated, the glory of victory would go to Black Diamond rather than Bull Mitchell.

And now, at the rear of the old Shotgun Riley saloon, a rival sheet sprang into being. It was called the *Six-Shooter* and was edited by an angular, squint-eyed, tobacco-stained individual whose sole recommendation to Bull Mitchell was the fact that he had, for five years, edited an eastern prison newspaper.

His name was Klink and he had done time for blackmail in connection with a periodical he had published in the east. The main source of income derived from that scandal sheet was not from its extensive circulation so much as it was from lack of circulation. Klink would get out a few private editions which were sent by messenger (thus avoiding arrest for misuse of the United States mails) to certain prominent men who would pay Klink, in unmarked cash, for the suppression of certain items of scandalous nature. Klink had done well until a New York banker had trapped him. Pete Smyth had known Klink in New York where the latter had become notorious among the spenders who made up the night life.

"I see you're out, Klink." Pete Smyth had ignored the proffered hand. For among newspaper men, Klink had long ago become a pariah. And that brotherhood is more than merely tolerant of man's faults. Pete ran a few lines under the *Assay's* death column.

We have among us [ran the bit] Ambrose Klink, formerly of New York, later of Sing Sing, where he has been enjoying a ten-year sojourn, expenses paid by a generous government. Moccasin Tracks, our reporter, informs us that Mr. Klink is to edit a sheet aptly named the *Six-Shooter*, office of that paper to be the rear of the Shotgun Riley Saloon. Not a bad location, considering. I could suggest but one better spot for any publication edited by Ambrose Klink. That location would be the small out-house in the rear of the saloon.

Pay Dirt, literally on its tiptoes to view the first edition of the *Six-Shooter*, was amply rewarded for its waiting. Almost the entire space of the paper was devoted to the history of Joe Morgan. Beginning with the boldly emblazoned fact that Wade Morgan was his father and had never honored Hattie Morgan by the ceremony of marriage, it dwelt upon the career of Wade Morgan as a killer, and cold-blooded bandit.

It gave a garbled version of Shotgun Riley's death. It branded Joe's mother as a bad woman. Long Bob was the easygoing, gullible fool who had assumed an unwanted burden and was undoubtedly sharing Wade Morgan's stolen loot as payment. . . .

How will you feel, you men and women of Pay Dirt, when some one outside the county taunts you with the fact that your district attorney is the illegitimate son of a notorious outlaw? That the son of a bad man and a fallen woman holds the reigns of the law in his hands? Supposing Wade Morgan or some of Wade Morgan's friends should come up for trial? Will this young tough, who in the memory of most of our citizens beat a man unconscious while Wade Morgan held a gun ready to kill Joe Morgan's enemy, should he be unfortunate enough to win, I ask you, men and women of Pay Dirt, will this young bully send Wade Morgan or any friend of Wade Morgan to prison? He will not.

Before the first edition of the *Six-Shooter* was given to the public, a messenger brought the first copy to Joe Morgan's office. Joe was there. So were Amy Steele, Pete Smyth, and Doc.

Joe, his face terribly white, read its accusations, its ugly slurs. Doc Steele, anticipating Joe's next move, blocked the way to the desk drawer that held his gun.

Pete Smyth had picked up a typed note that had come with the paper. He read it, smiled thinly, and handed it to Joe who stood there, trying to regain his self-control. Almanac and Kit Kavanaugh—Kit was now the Pay Dirt Schoolma'am —came in.

Joe Morgan read the unsigned note, his jaw jutting stubbornly. Pete plucked the bit of paper from Joe's hand and read it aloud.

"Withdraw from the fight and the *Six-Shooter*, lock, stock and barrel, including its first edition, becomes yours in exchange for one dollar."

"I'll ram his filthy sheet down his throat," said Joe huskily. "I expected to be given a lot of abuse on account of my father. But when a yellow-backed cur like Ambrose Klink or Bull Mitchell fouls the name of my mother, there's only one thing for me to do and still call myself a man."

"Meaning," said Pete Smyth, with that same thin smile that was not a smile, "that you intend getting your gat and stalking across the street. Josephus, my lad, getting yourself killed is exactly in keeping with their program. You wouldn't have a skunk's chance. I'll prove it. Kitten, would you mind stepping over to yonder den of iniquity and asking Casey the time of day or the day of the month or why does a chicken cross the road or some other equally vital question? You,

Almanac, stay here. Kit does a solo and she don't need the accompaniment of a .45. And while thus engaged with friend Casey, while brother Klink and fellow-citizens Mitchell, Love, Patchens, *et al.*, are gathered about, kindly mention, by way of conversation, small-talk, and repartee as we find it on page nine of 'How to Be a Riot Where Once You Were a Bore,' kindly mention, Kitten, that Joe Morgan would not give a dollar for the *Six-Shooter*, even if they threw in Klink and Black Diamond by the way of boot."

"Look here, Pete, you can't let Kit—" Joe made a helpless gesture as Kit blew them a kiss and left the office.

"Don't worry about Kit, Joe. She's the only one of us who can step across the street without starting a civil war. Son, this is going to be a battle. A bitter, nasty scrap. Give the queen of Whisky Gulch all the credit for the dirt that's on that sheet. Bull's a tough baby, but he's not that cowardly. Fact is, I got it from Moccasin Tracks that Bull raised particular hob when the queen insisted on dragging in Mrs. Burch. But she made Bull lie down and play dead. She has something on the Bullock, I'm thinking. Moccasin Tracks also informs me that Patchen, Klink, and some other thugs are waiting across there for you to come over and play in their back yards."

"Who is Moccasin Tracks, anyhow?" asked Doc.

"Moccasin Tracks is our spy in the enemy camp. Sorry, Doc, but I can't enlighten you further. Because, if the spy's identity became known, Moccasin Tracks would go out like a candle in a gale. Here comes Kit."

Amy Steele felt a twinge of something akin to jealousy as she watched Kit Kavanaugh, trim and athletic and boyish-looking in tailored riding breeches and English boots, stride along with an unconscious swagger, hands deep in her pockets, whistling an Irish jig.

"Well," she told them airly, "the war's on. Half a dozen breed kids are already out peddling papers. A big stack went into the mail. And Joe, those coyotes were ready and waiting, as Pete said they'd be, to make you over into a nice corpse. And if you don't win this election, Joe Morgan, I'm sunk. I just bet ten thousand bucks on you. Also bet the *Assay* against the *Six-Shooter*. Now let's elect some campaign managers and outline a plan. Doc, you'll have to get a substitute to take my place at school until election's over. Because Pete Smyth has to manage Joe and I have to ride close herd on Pete and Almanac."

"Amy can take over the school," nodded Doc. "And while

we're here together, there's something I want to ask you. I need your combined opinion. I've already sounded out a good many solid citizens and they think as I do. Men, I propose Bob Burch for sheriff."

There was a moment of silence. There was a queer expression on the leathery face of old Almanac as he and Joe Morgan exchanged glances. Doc Steele rightly interpreted their nods of dissent.

"When it's put to Bob the right way, boys, I think he'll see the situation as I see it. The name of Long Bob Burch has always been linked with Wade Morgan's name. Bob is accused of being a silent member of the outlaw gangs. That is a lie. Bob Burch is an honest man, an honorable man, and a man who will stand for real justice. The time has come when men like Sim Patchen must go. Patchen, and other officers like Patchen, breed contempt for the law. But if a strong man is put into office, we'll support him and help him bring law and order into this county. Bob Burch is the man for the job."

"He'll never take it, Doc," said Almanac.

"No harm to feel him out," maintained Pete Smyth, "and it looks to me like Doc is the right party to approach him."

"Doc and Kit," amended Almanac. "Bob thinks a heap of Kit. I'll git Bob up to her house this evenin'. Then her an' Doc kin stretch him out an' put the law an order iron on his ribs."

"Bring him up for supper. You're all invited. Roast beef and brown gravy. Pumpkin pie. A good cigar. Gosh, Pete, I believe we have a fighting chance of putting it over on poor Bob. Since he's been left alone, he has sort of lost interest. He's lonesome, without anything or anybody to work for. The job would be a blessing in disguise."

"Disguise is right," added Joe. "Bob never thought much of sheriffs."

"Because there were too many like Patchen. Bought and paid for by men like Bull Mitchell. Bounty hunters." Doc turned to Amy. "Corral Bob and see that he shows up for supper. Tell him it's his birthday. He's down at the postoffice talking politics with Uncle Duffy." Uncle Duffy was the post-master of Pay Dirt.

"If you find him reading the post-cards," Pete put in, "that cinches the bet. He's the logical man for sheriff. A Sherlock Holmes type." Pete consulted his watch. Almanac did likewise. Kit looked at Joe's clock and nodded. The two scribes made a dignified but hasty exit.

"I've pulled them on a schedule," Kit explained. "It's now

their third drink hour. I hope you've noticed, Doc, that Pete has put on weight. And neither of them have been tight for six months. Did you know that if Pete stayed like he is now, he could hold down the editor's desk in any one a dozen of the biggest newspapers in the country? Yet, I dread the day when Pete will tire of Pay Dirt and go back east. It will be like a man going to prison."

"You seem to have a pet grudge against the big cities," smiled Doc.

Kit's smile returned. "New York or San Francisco are bad medicine for some people, Doc. Pete's one of 'em. As for me, I've adopted this country. In later years, if you see a bent, white-haired old lady puttering about in a garden, growing roses and onions and packing an ear trumpet, that'll be Kit Kavanaugh. Doc, take Joe for a walk or a ride or down to Tex's for a game of freeze-out. Show up at my wigwam at six sharp for a cocktail and supper and then we'll hogtie Long Bob."

Kit left the two men there. Joe Morgan balled up the copy of Klink's *Six-Shooter* and tossed it into the waste basket. "Beats the devil how that girl can drive away gloom, Doc."

"A most remarkable girl, Joe. She'll make some lucky man a splendid wife." He took Joe's arm and the two men walked down the street to Tex Calhoun's.

When Kit reached her cabin, she sat down and wrote a four-page letter. Its envelope bore the name and address of a well-known gambler in Hot Springs, Arkansas. The envelope inside bore no name. The gambler would see that it eventually reached Wade Morgan. This done, Kit busied herself with the supper that was to pave the way for the conspiracy.

So it came about that Long Bob Burch accepted the nomination for sheriff, to run against Sim Patchen.

That supper at Kit Kavanaugh's held another surprise. Joe Morgan and Amy Steele announced the fact that they were going to be married some time after the election.

Chapter Fifteen

FREE DRINKS

BEN THRASHER, candidate for district attorney, knew law. He saw to it that Ambrose Klink did not overstep certain limits. The wily Klink stayed within the law and still managed to put across certain yellow propaganda that was hurting Joe

Morgan's chances of election. He had the knack of putting certain facts, harmless facts, into words that made those facts sound differently.

Joe Morgan saw defeat in the offing. It was apparent to all that Bob Burch would share that defeat. Even the optimistic Pete Smyth was forced to admit that Klink was undermining the chances of Joe Morgan and Long Bob Burch. People were afraid to vote for two men so closely linked with such a man as Wade Morgan.

"I see you've changed the *Assay* office into a nice little morgue," announced Kit Kavanaugh.

"We're thinking of putting Doc Steele up for coroner so that at least one man on our ticket will get an office," said Pete gloomily. "No sane man wants the coroner job and there's only one man who will accept it. That's Peg Leg. Peg Leg enjoys looking at dead men. Ho hum." He glanced meaningly at his watch. "Where's Almanac?"

"Almanac has gone on an errand. He'll be back to-morrow night. You'll have to make your next few drinks Dick Smiths."

"A cowardly trick, Kitten. A scurvy deal, I calls it. You know I never drink alone."

"Never?"

"Well, hardly ever. Where'd you send brother Almanac?"

"On an errand. Pete, have you any connections at the state capital? I don't mean bartenders or tramps. Think hard."

"There's . . . lemme think now . . . yeh, there's my good friend Blinkey. And Gloomy Jake."

"Comedy team at some beer hall?"

"Quite the contrary, my dear young lady. You insult my integrity and malign my friends. I speak of two friends of my youth. Two gentlemen of honor and principle, two knights of—"

"Never mind the speech. Who are these crooks?"

"Crooks? If you were a man, and not too able bodied, I would challenge you to a duel, nothing less. I speak of two men prominent in the affairs of state. State senators, nothing less."

"Honest, Pete?"

"Honest Injun, Kitten."

"Could you ask them a favor without being given the bum's rush?"

"Again your sex and age protect you. I could ask them any sort of favor—" Pete lit another cigarette—"and the favor would be granted. Kid Aladdin and his trick lamp had nothing on Peter Bartholomew Smyth. Y as in Why not."

"Then drag your Sunday duds out of the mothballs and get a haircut. Be ready to go to Helena to-morrow evening. And ask no questions, because I've been trying to quit lying, even though I am sort of assistant politician."

And when she had left the two men staring after her, Pete turned to Joe, his low spirits gone.

"There," announced the newspaper man, with a profound gesture, "goes a woman who is a paragon. Beautiful as the dawn, clever as a magician, and a marvelous cook. Besides being blessed with such attributes as virtue, wit, the biggest heart in the world, and her own bank account. Were I twenty years younger I would devote my life to crawling about, here and there, after her, upon my bleeding knees, begging her to marry me. Joe, the Kitten has an ace in the hole. Let's amble down the main stem and crook our elbows while exchanging choice bits of wisdom with brother Buford. He opened a new bottle of twenty-year-old stuff no later than this morning. My private bottle. We shall drink a toast to Kit Kavanaugh, chip off the old block of Kilkenny Kavanaughs. Or is it County Kerry that boasts of such stock? And we shall stand there, heads bowed in silence, in sorrow, as we think of the absent Almanac who is missing one."

As they strolled down the street in an almost cheerful mood, Bill Clanton rode up the street and dismounted in front of the Shotgun Riley saloon that now bore a huge banner labeled,

CAMPAIGN HEADQUARTERS
FREE DRINKS AND FREE LUNCH

"First time that gobbler has fouled the village with his odorous presence in some time," observed Pete. "A bearer of important tidings or I'm a hunchback follower of Carrie Nation."

"He's come a long ways," said Joe, noting the condition of Clanton's sweat-streaked, spur-marked horse. "You can bet it's important, Pete. That old woman of his wouldn't let him come to town alone, otherwise."

"Moccasin Tracks will get the low-down before long."

Pete led the way to Tex Buford's bar. The big saloon man shoved a copy of the Great Falls paper at Pete.

"Wade's done cut loose again," he told Joe Morgan. "Held up a gambling house in Butte. A one-man job. He'd bin playin' poker all night. Claimed the dealer was crooked and he'd taken the dealer's roll. Never bothered nobody else. Told 'em to stay outa the play because he didn't want to hurt nobody. That was four nights ago. Doggone, Joe, when yuh git in office, do somethin' about gittin' a better mail service out here. Twict a week ain't enough fer a city like Pay Dirt."

"You'll be getting mail twice a day, Tex, by the time I get in office," said Joe, a little bitterly. "This settles my hash. All I'll get now is the family vote."

"Too bad Wade didn't put it off till after election," agreed Tex. "He would, if he'd knowed, Joe." He slid out a squat brown bottle and three glasses. Pete folded the paper and handed it back to Tex.

"Beats hell how the weather keeps up," he said gloomily, and filled his glass to the brim.

As the three of them stood there at the bar, wrapped in a depressing silence, Sim Patchen and two of Bull Mitchell's toughs strode past and on down to the feed barn. All three were armed with Winchesters. A few minutes later other of Mitchell's cohorts followed suit, among them Bill Clanton on a fresh horse.

Pete Smyth excused himself and went out the back door. In about half an hour he rejoined Joe and Tex. Pete's face carried an expression of deeper gloom, mixed with consternation.

"Bill Clanton brought in word that Wade Morgan had been seen down near the mouth of Rock Creek. He's camped back in the breaks. Sim Patchen sees an opportunity to cinch his election if he can slip down there and kill Wade Morgan. Perhaps you men can see some sort of a silver lining in that cloud?"

"Wade might kill Sim Patchen," offered Tex.

"Which would rid us of a skunk but would come a hell of a long ways from putting Joe and Long Bob in office. It's thumbs down for us, Joe. Tex, let's have another look at that bottle. Kit will understand the dire necessity. Though I'll admit it'll take a damn sight more than a corkscrew to pull us out of this hole."

It was a pair of sorrow-laden politicians who made their way up to Kit's for supper.

"Why don't some one whistle the dead march?" she asked them scornfully. "Pete Smyth, about face. Hit a lope for that barber shop and get a haircut and shave. I've got your clothes laid out and your bag packed. We'll use Bob Burch's team and the top buggy. We may pull out any time after dark. I think Almanac will be back sooner than I figured. And get word to your mysterious Moccasin Tracks that Black Diamond is getting darned suspicious. Trot, Pete. Be back in twenty minutes. And tell that hair carpenter to do a better job than

he did last time. That old bowl-and-scissors cut is out of date."
She shoved him out the door. "Trot. Lope. Hit a run!"

Kit turned to Joe, who had slumped down in a chair and
reached for a bottle of Scotch that stood on the smoking
stand.

"I'll pour." Kit took the bottle and filled two glasses.

"Why two drinks? Pete's gone."

"Your drink, Joe." She handed him his filled glass. "The
other one is mine."

"I thought you never touched liquor, Kit?"

"This will be the first drink I've ever taken in my life, Joe."

"I don't think, Kit, that I quite understand. Why are you
taking that drink?"

"Because," she told him, biting each word off sharply, "it
seems to be the custom hereabouts to get drunk when the
breaks are going against one. I'm tired and worried sick and
bluer than indigo and don't give a damn if I die. So I'm going
to ape you and Pete Smyth and get drunk. Here's to crime!"

She lifted the glass. Joe's swift blow sent it spinning across
the room, spilling the contents on a thick rug. Then he tossed
his own drink into the fireplace. He walked over to where she
was standing and took her two hands in his.

"Thanks, Kit. I was being a yellow quitter. For the past
week and more I've moped around, drinking too much, expecting you to come along and cheer me up. I've been a
damned coward, Kit. And you've been game. More game than
any man I ever knew."

For the first time, Joe Morgan saw the tired, harassed lines
about her mouth. There were hollow circles of blue under her
eyes. He realized that for all her swagger and flippancy, she
was just a girl—a girl who hid her own burdens under a cloak
of gallantry.

Suddenly Joe took her in his arms. His lips found hers,
kissed them hungrily. Kit's arms were about his neck, her
mouth eager for his kisses. For a long moment neither of them
moved. Kit lay like a very tired child in his embrace and his face
was buried in her hair.

They did not hear the door open. Nor did they see Amy
Steele enter. Amy, white as ice, stood there, just inside the
threshold. She made no sound. Blank horror was replaced by
a look of bitter accusation. She felt very calm and self-possessed.

"I beg your most humble pardon for so rudely interrupting
such a delightful little love scene," she said coldly, "and I
should have withdrawn and left you both none the wiser for
my untimely visit. But I hate anything underhanded or sneak-

ing, so I chose to stay and let you know I've found you out, both of you. Any one but a simple country girl would have long ago guessed that your friendship was more than platonic. Here's your ring, Joe. I won't be hypocrite enough to wish you happiness because I now dislike you, Kit Kavanaugh, as much as you've always disliked me. And for the same reason."

She tossed her engagement ring on the table, smiled crookedly, and went out.

Joe, his face scarlet, stood there like a man stricken dumb. Kit dropped into a chair.

"I'm going to either weep or laugh like a fool. Or both. For the love of Mike, Joe, take a drink or whistle or bawl me out for a hussy or something. Take a swing at me or kiss me or do a song or dance. Joe, I'm—I'm all in."

And Kit Kavanaugh fainted for the first time in her life.

Chapter Sixteen

TWO-GUN KIT

PETE SMYTH returned from the barber shop to find Kit all alone. Her eyes showed signs of recent tears. "What's the ruckus, Kitten? Where's Joe?"

"I sent Joe for a long walk, Pete. Hence, the teary eyes. I'll be all right in a jiffy. Pete, did you ever want something awfully bad? So bad that you kept thinking of it all day and dreaming about it at night? And you tightened up your belt and went after it with all your might. Then you saw it slip out of your hands and you had to sit back and smile and kid yourself into thinking it was God's will or just one of the breaks of the game or something. Then, when you'd almost whipped that longing for something beyond your reach, when you'd quit crying for the moon, Pete, it's handed to you on a gold platter—with trimmings. You bounce from hell and crash the gates of Paradise. You feel like Cinderella or something. Your pumpkins are fine carriages, Pete. Oh, God, it's like a miracle, Pete. Queen for an hour. But you're stealing your throne. You're cheating. Using a marked deck in a friendly, honorable· game. . . . I'm mixing up my similes and all, but you savvy.

"I just gave Joe Morgan the gate, Pete. He took me in his arms and kissed me. Then, like some dizzy stage play, Pete, who should walk in but Amy. And she said her lines without stuttering once. Nary a lisp, Pete. And when she had told us, with words and with looks that were like daggers, no less, she made her exit. And I, like some frail damsel of King Arthur's court, I actually swooned. Honest, Pete. Simply went out like a blind eye, no less. And when I came out of it, there was Joe, holding me tight, telling me over and over that he loved, me. And I'd be a darned liar if I said I didn't like it like a kid likes Christmas.

"Pete, if I'd been a spectator and had watched it all from the sidelines, I'd have sworn that the whole thing was framed. That slick city gal, the lady of shady fame, had simply pulled a fast one on the simple swain betrothed to the pure little country lass. That this city slicker had played lady-spider. And maybe I did, Pete. Maybe, subconsciously, I trapped Joe into falling for me. Women are queer animals. But I really didn't do it on purpose.

"I told you once, ages ago, that I wanted Joe Morgan. I meant it, with all my heart. I thoroughly disliked Amy Steele because I knew she loved Joe and had shared his boyhood. I even told her that I disliked her. And the poor kid didn't know why. She tried her best to make me like her. And I hated her for it. Then, last winter, when she and I worked with the sick people, when we shared the same bed and meals and sorrows and work, I forgot to hate her. And in the end I liked her, Pete, more than I've ever let myself like any woman. I saw that, under that shy, almost insipid paleness of character, she was big and wonderful and sweet and kind and everything. She trusted me, Pete, and she drove out of my heart a lot of the cynical bitterness that the other women had put there. She was like my kid sister. I knew she loved Joe. She'd always loved him. And so I went up on the mountain one day and had a long talk with myself. 'Kit,' says I to myself, 'you've two courses. Either blow town tomorrow or else stay here and make yourself forget about wanting Joe Morgan.' Well, I chose the latter course."

"Because you thought Joe Morgan and Pete Smyth and others needed you." Pete put in. "Go on, Kitten."

"I stayed, Pete. And I thought I had it whipped. . . . until this evening. I was low and blue and tired. Like a groggy fighter. And the minute I felt his lips kissing mine, I knew that I would always love Joe Morgan. He was the first man in my life. He'd be the last."

"Poor little old Kitten."

"Don't Pete. I can't stand it just now. . . . So when I came awake after taking the count, I did what I could to repair the damage. I sent Joe back to Amy. He'll feel like an idiot and she'll always hate me, but they'll patch it up and get married and she'll have his babies and they'll sit in front of the fire and get a good laugh out of it all some day."

"You mean to tell me, Kitten, that you wouldn't take Joe, even when he told you he loved you?"

"Perhaps he was just swept off his feet, Pete. Amy's his girl. She's always been his sweetheart, since they were youngsters. Their love is the comfortable kind. Solid, without much emotion. They wouldn't quarrel once in a green moon. They belong to one another. So I gave him back to Amy."

"What did you tell Joe? How did you make him willing to give you up? The truth now, Kitten."

"It was easy enough. What's the most dangerous weapon a person can use, Pete? Ridicule, of course. And I used it. I laughed at him. Made him believe that I was just playing with him. Like I played with lots of other men who kissed me. I let him think, Pete, that . . . well, that it wasn't the first time I was willing to love a man . . . providing the price was right. . . . Naturally, he took his hat and left."

"You did that, Kit?" asked Pete Smyth, his voice harsh. "You made him think you were a common woman who was for hire? You, *you*, my Kitten, did that? You told that damned lie?"

Pete turned toward the door. Kit pulled him back.

"Don't, Pete. I know you want to go after Joe and bring him back and make me admit I lied. I know I've hurt you as much as I've hurt Joe. But Pete, honey, it's just one of the breaks. It was my last card and I played it for an ace. Joe will never repeat what I told him. What if he did? It would only go a little ways further in strengthening the suspicions of others. Who believes I'm really decent? You and Dad. Dad's dead."

Kit lit a cigarette. Her hands were steady now. She pushed Pete into a chair and perched herself on his lap, mussing his hair and pulling his ears and laughing at him.

"How old are you, Pete?"

"About forty. Why?"

"Good teeth, hair white but nice and thick. Riding and hiking and sobriety has put meat on you. You're handsomer than most men. You're the cleverest man I ever met. You've been a dad and mother and big brother to me. I'm awfully proud of you. I think more of you than any other man, except Joe Morgan. And when this darn election is over, I'm going away. A year from now I'll have forgotten it all. Pete, I dare you to marry me and take me back to New York."

"Marry you? Good God, Kit, you're crazy!"

"All of us are a little loco, according to these trick brain experts. And you surely do need a wife, Pete. Why, Pete, we'd be happier than two donkeys that have broken into a grain field. We know how to play together. We understand one another. With me to anchor you, you can go to the top. We'll have a country home, a place at the beach, some dogs and good saddle horses—"

Kit's face colored. She had almost added children to the list. And Pete, who knew her better than any one in the world knew Kit Kavanaugh deliberately kept silent.

Kit took his lean, tanned face in her hands and kissed him on the mouth.

"Yes, Pete, she said gently, "and a couple of youngsters."

"If it will make you happy, Kit, I'll take you up on that bet."

"Just for that, you can have one more drink. A small one. Then get into the tub. As soon as Almanac shows up, we may be on our way. And Pete, dear, for the love of Jupiter, wash that smelly junk off your hair. How many times have I told you not to let that nit-wit barber use that bay rum? You smell like the professor at Black Diamond's dance hall."

"What's this trip to Helena all about?"

"Election. We're going to put Bob Burch and Joe Morgan in office. Pete, we've just begun to fight. Wait till you scoop this for the *Assay*."

Kit sat down at the piano. Pete Smyth, in the bath-tub, paused to listen. Kit was singing softly, playing her own accompaniment. The song was an old Irish love song that had been her father's favorite. It was a melody, the plaintive chords of which were sad and sweet. The heart strings of Ireland. Dreams put into muted music of a harp. Only an Irishman blessed with an Irishman's gift for dreaming, could have composed it. Only Kathleen Mavoureen Kavanaugh could have sung it thus. And only Pete Smyth, blessed and cursed with a dreamer's understanding, could know the heart of the singer.

After a cold shower, Pete Smyth dressed. For the first time since he had come to pay Dirt, he put on his tailored clothes, his custom-made shirt, English-built shoes. Tanned, muscular, clear-eyed. His prematurely whitened hair was thick and wavy and was cropped to a finely made head. Kit had spoken no more than the truth when she called him a handsome man. He was twenty pounds heavier than he had been since his college days when the name of Pete Smyth meant something in college athletics. He went into the front room.

Kit spent five whole minutes telling him how splendid he looked. She fussed over him, adjusted an already perfect tie. She got a whisk-broom and brushed him. Her eyes danced with excitement. Kit had never seen him looking so fit. Somehow, she had always thought of Pete as an old man, pale and dissipated, a derelict. His hair had been gray since she could remember. But this was no wreck.

"Gee, Pete! Gosh! If you ever spoil this picture for me, I'll have you hung, so help me, Hiram."

She was dressed in a severely-tailored brown traveling suit. From the tips of her brown suede pumps to the crown of her copper-hued hair, Kit was perfect. They were acting like two kids when Almanac, dust-covered and weary-looking, swung from his saddle and came into the room without the formality of rapping. His blue eyes blinked with astonishment. But he answered Kit's mute question.

"Everything's set, ma'am. The rest is up to you."

"Almanac," said Kit, "you're a winner. A champ. What a whipping we'll give Bull Mitchell! Help yourself to the Scotch. Then wash up and I'll rustle your supper while Pete gets the team hooked up. Not a word to any one, Pete. Tell 'em we're eloping or blowing the burg or something."

While Kit piled Almanac's plate with food and opened a bottle of beer for him, the old cowpuncher talked. Talked in a low tone, while Kit listened to his every word.

Pete drove up. Kit gripped Almanac's shoulder tightly. "Wash the dishes or stack 'em. Get as tight as you like. And do your sleeping here. Use the spare bed. Tell Bob and Joe to sit tight until we get back. Mum's the word. Don't forget to eat while I'm gone. There's plenty in the cooler. A cold roast of beef, potato salad, and two apple pies. So-long."

Chapter Seventeen

THE HAT

TWO days later Kit Kavanaugh and Pete Smyth returned to Pay Dirt. Almanac met them at the feed barn and walked up the street with them, carrying Kit's bag. They stopped at the *Assay* office. Almanac brought in Long Bob and Joe. Joe, a little white and strained-looking, tried to return Kit's smile, but his effort was a miserable failure. He looked as if he needed sleep.

But Kit ignored his half sullen embarrassment. She took

a nickle badge from her handbag and handed it to Bob Burch. "Pin it on where it'll show. You are now a U. S. special deputy marshal. I've got the papers, properly signed, to prove it. The stage is all set. It's up to you to step into the limelight and knock the populace for the count. And please try to grin. You know darned well that everything is all right or Almanac wouldn't be party to it. Here it is, in headlines, in the Helena paper and the Great Falls *Tribune* and the *Leader*. Wade's letter word for word. His promise to surrender to one man and only one man. The man is none other than Bob Burch, U. S. Deputy Marshal."

Joe Morgan leaped from his chair, his eyes blazing. "What the devil is this, anyhow?" His voice was shaking with rage. "What fool's idea is all this damned rot?"

"Keep yore shirt on, Little Britches," growled Almanac.

"What's the meaning of all this idiocy?" Joe Morgan faced them, white with fury. "I won't be a party to such a—"

"Dry up," snapped Almanac. "You aint got a damn thing tuh say, nohow. Serve yuh right if yuh got beat at election. Keep yore shirt on. Me'n Wade Morgan an' Bob has talked 'er all over. Bob's a-goin' after Wade to-night. He'll take him tuh jail at Helena. Wade's in bad shape, account of his lungs and some old bullet wounds that's a-botherin' him. He's quit the Wild Bunch because he's slowed up so bad he can't foller 'em no more. They shipped him off to the Argentine but he come back. He wants tuh die here at home. He's givin' hisse'f up tuh Bob and me to-night."

"He'll die in jail, then, or prison, or be hung," said Joe bitterly. "He'll be tried first for the killing of Shotgun Riley. If I'm elected to the office of district attorney, it'll be up to me to prosecute the case. I'll be sending my own father to the pen. I'll be his murderer." He swung his accusing eyes to Kit. His finger shook in her face. "You've done this. You and Pete Smyth! What the hell do you want to come here for meddling in other people's business, ruining lives, just for the sake of excitement? I wish to God I'd never—"

"That'll do, Joe." Long Bob Burch's voice was low pitched, compelling. Joe went suddenly silent.

"It was Wade's idea, Joe," Burch went on, almost gently. "It's his way of doing something for us all. Wade's changed. Changed a heap, since I'd seen him last. He's an old man, Joe. Old and broken-down, and plumb alone. He's traveled too fast and too hard and he wants tuh quit runnin' like a coyote. It's all in his letter he wrote to Kit a long time ago. And Joe, don't go callin' Kit hard names. It's through her and a friend of her father's that Wade's bin took care of fer more than a year, now. Down in the south, at a high-toned sanitarium. Her money footed the bills, and you can bet them bills was plenty big. Her letters has bin cheerin' him up, helpin' him live. She wrote him every week. Wade told me all about it and it's the only time I ever seen him weaken and act soft. He busted plumb down. Cried like a kid. No, Joe, I wouldn't be callin' this girl no hard names." Long Bob turned to Almanac. "We better be pullin' out. Doc'll be wonderin' if somethin's gone wrong."

Kit pinned his new badge to the lapel of his coat.

"We had better luck than I dared hope, there in Helena," she said. "Wade won't even step inside the jail. He'll go to the hospital. Under guard, of course, but it won't be jail. Thank Pete for that. He did himself proud. Imagine him call-ing these terribly dignified men Blinky and Gloomy Jake. And the editor of the Helena *Record* held half of the front page open for Pete's story. Then they got out an extra to catch the overflow. It's the biggest story that's broke in years. If the jury ever reads it they'll turn Wade Morgan loose and run him for senator. Give my best regards to Wade. And give him the package I left in the buggy. It's fruit. Strawberries, mostly, because he likes 'em. And some fifty-cent cigars. Com-pliments of Pete Smyth. And get back here by next Tuesday to help celebrate your election."

When Long Bob and Almanac had gone, Kit crossed over to Joe Morgan, who sat there, a baffled sort of look in his eyes.

"Don't take it like that, Joe. Can't you understand how we just had to keep you in the dark? You'd have spoiled the whole thing. Wade is trying to do this for you because you're his son and he's darned proud of you. He wants you to be a big man, a really big man. You're riding a lot of fool notions just now. Quit it. You're going into office without a doubt in the world. It's a cinch. And that's only the first round of the big fight ahead of you. Some day we'll be saying, 'I knew that gent when he was nothing but a two-bit lawyer in a little country town.' Joe, you're going to be a great man some day. When you are, remember to-day."

"You make a man feel like a school kid that's been caught cheating at a spelling-bee, Kit. I feel cheap and little and silly."

"Sure you do. And Pete will back me up when I say that

it's all in the molding of something big. Character-building, little grains of sand into mountains grow. Little drops of water into . . . etcetera and son on. Have you seen Amy?"

"No."

"Just as I thought. Pete, go down to Tex's. Take exactly three drinks. Allow a minute between each drink. When they hit your toes, trot over to the schoolhouse, tell Amy Steele that there's a half holiday this afternoon. Then take her for a walk. Walk her up the mountain till you come to a big flat rock. She'll be out of breath by then and be unable to interrupt you. When your lecture is over, and she's sort of stunned, as it were, slip away. Then you can come back and get a nice glow on before supper."

Pete grinned, took Joe's hand and pumped it with fervent vigor, kissed Kit, and was gone. Joe sat stupefied. Kit lit a cigarette, walked about, humming a little as she straightened a littered desk, opened some letters addressed to the Pay Dirt *Assay*, and finally paused at a husky word from Joe.

"Kit!"

"Yes?"

"I wish you'd tell me, Kit, that you lied the other night about what you told me."

"Let's not go into that again, Joe. Please. We were both a little mad that evening. Moonstruck, loco. I want you to marry Amy, Joe. When Pete returns here, I want you to streak it up that trail to the big flat rock. Don't come down until that engagement ring is back on Amy's finger."

"But, Kit, I don't love—"

"Of course you love Amy. Don't be a dunce. You've always loved her and she's worshipped you. That's what Pete will be telling her in a few minutes. And take it from me, any man that can talk a governor into pardoning Wade Morgan, can convince a girl like Amy Steele that her heart ain't even cracked, to say nothing of being busted.

"Pete got the governor to sign Wade Morgan's pardon?" gasped Joe.

"Not exactly, but words to that effect. Wade Morgan is slowly dying. For his crimes, he has been punished. A large percentage of the money he stole has been refunded, never mind how. In return for that, and certain other things, I think it will be so arranged that Wade Morgan will die outside the gray shadows of prison walls. Perhaps at his old home ranch."

"And I made a fool of myself, bawling you and Pete out!"

"Naturally. We both expected that. No hard feelings. If

you hadn't been so terribly het up, you'd have seen us both grinning. . . . You'll be a good boy and make it all up with Amy?"

"I want you to tell me, Kit," said Joe stubbornly, "that you lied when you told me you were bad. I know down in my heart that you deliberately lied, but I want to hear you say so."

"Anything to get along. I lied Joe."

"Then tell me, Kit, that your kisses meant—"

"Meant nothing, Joe except that I was hysterical." She held out her left hand. On its third finger was a beautiful solitaire. "I'm marrying Pete Smyth, Joe."

"You love him, Kit?"

"I've always loved him, Joe. Now, will you go up and tell Amy that she can't leave that rock till she promises to be your wife?"

"Yes." Joe got to his feet. He held out his hand. Kit took it in both of hers. Her hands were cold.

"I want you and Pete to be happy, Kit. . . . Mighty happy. Life owes it to you both."

"Kiss me, Joe. Just once. Just once, for happiness. Then climb your rock and find Amy. She'll be there on the big flat rock. It's my Wishing Rock, Joe."

Joe kissed her gravely, without passion. Then he went out almost colliding with Pete, who was whistling gaily and seemed in a festive mood. Again Pete gripped Joe's hand and pumped it vigorously.

"She's up there, Joe. The stage is all set. Enter, the hero. Dum, dum de dum. Let 'er buck!"

When Joe had departed, Kit and Pete faced one another.

"Is there anything in this' world, Pete, that you would refuse to do for me?"

"Nothing in this world, nor beyond it, Kitten," came the quick reply.

"If any other man said that," said Kit, her eyes soft with emotion, "I'd take it simply as a very pretty compliment. But you really mean it. It almost frightens me, Pete."

"Nonsense, Kitten. What, ho? Opening my mail, eh? Jealous, I bet." He sorted out some letters. "Bill, another bill, letter from the *Tribune*, that one's from Wally Hoffman of the Denver *Post*, a note from the *Chronicle*, and another from New York. Ties that are tugging at the old heart, Kit, pulling me back into the city. Back into the harness again. Into the bustle and grind and rewards and grief of the game. In a few more weeks, Kit, we'll be back among 'em."

He puffed hard at his pipe, his eyes staring at his littered desk as if he saw another desk set back in a niche in a big newspaper office. And Kit followed his thoughts. Minutes of silence, broken by the song of a meadowlark outside. Pete's eyes met Kit's.

"Why the devil aren't we tickled green at the prospect of going back where we belong, tell me an answer to that, Kitten?"

"I haven't an answer, Pete. I don't know why I dread going back to the big towns. I just can't kick up any enthusiasm over it."

"Nor can I. Odd, I calls it, shipmate. I don't particularly like it here. When we've licked brother Mitchell, and put Joe and Long Bob in office, it's going to be too darned quiet and monotonous around here. I'll get stale. It'll be too doggoned decent and humdrum. No items for the Boot Hill column. No fights, no nothing. In reforming Pay Dirt, we're sapping the place of its color. Ho hum. How about a game of cut-throat poker, just you and I? While we await the triumphant return of friend Joe?"

Pete Smyth loved to see Kit Kavanaugh's strong white hands manipulate cards. He was terribly proud of her cleverness. He was watching her deal crooked poker, trying to catch her at cheating, when Joe came in alone.

"Amy wasn't there, Pete. Her hat was on the rock, but she'd gone." Joe tossed the hat on the desk. It was a white felt hat with a blue ribbon. Kit picked it up, idly examinging it. Joe seemed a little glad that he had not found Amy there. The awkward meeting was postponed.

Vaguely, Kit was wondering how Amy Steele, usually so immaculate in her dress had worn a hat that was so noticeably soiled. Its brim bore some dark smudges, like marks left by soiled hands. But it was not until some hours later, when darkness found Amy missing, that Kit placed any value on the smudges that marred the white hat. A careless remark from Pete Smyth further alarmed Kit. Kit and Pete were getting out the next edition of the Pay Dirt *Assay*.

"Here's a local item of interest for the Lost and Found column, Kit. Moccasin Tracks slipped me the news that Tug and Tim Clanton have come back to the country. They were seen at their ranch the other day when the posse was hunting Wade."

Chapter Eighteen

KIT CROSSES THE DEADLINE

PETE," said Kit tensely, as she showed him the soiled white hat, "something horrible has happened to Amy Steele. I'm adding two plus two and getting ten, but I know my answer is right. Get hold of Doc Steele and Joe Morgan and any other men you can trust to keep their mouths shut. And while you're at it, see what else about the Clantons you can get from your Moccasin Tracks. I'm playing the hunch that the two Clanton whelps have kidnaped Amy Steele. Go at it mighty quietly, Pete, because this thing may turn out to be ugly before it's ended."

She examined her revolver. "Meet me at my house when you can, Pete."

"Where are you going now, Kit?"

"I'm paying a little party call. I have a hunch that Black Diamond can throw some light on this deal."

"You're not going across the street alone, Kit. Bull Mitchell hates you and so does his mulatto queen. They'd be glad of the chance to harm you."

"They don't care, Pete. Besides, I can handle myself even in tough company. And Moccasin Tracks will be around somewhere. Moccasin Tracks likes me."

"What do you know about Moccasin Tracks?"

"Everything, Pete. Now gather Doc and Joe and a few more we can trust. I'll be at the house in half an hour."

Kit Kavanaugh crossed the deadline and entered the Shotgun Riley saloon. The place was well packed with men and women. Tinny music blared. Smoke hung like gray curtains from the dingy ceiling and fly-spotted festoons. The bar was crowded. But neither Bull Mitchell nor Black Diamond were in evidence. Nobody noticed Kit as she opened the door that led into Bull Mitchell's private office. Nobody, that is, save Casey, who gave a quick start, as if to warn her away. But she had opened the door and had gone inside before the big bartender could stop her. He shrugged his thick shoulders and made sure that the big wooden mallet, better known as a bung-starter, was within easy reach. Then he carried on his business of serving thirsty customers.

Inside the small, box-like office, Kit Kavanaugh faced three persons. Bull Mitchell, Black Diamond, and Peg Leg Love. All three stared hard at the intruder. Kit smiled crookedly.

"Well," growled Bull, "what the hell do you want?"

"Just about five minutes of the queen's time, if she has the sand to face me alone."

"Get out, Bull," said Black Diamond, in her low-pitched, husky voice, "you and Peg Leg. I'll handle this little cat."

"Don't play the fool," rumbled Bull. "Let me handle her." He clenched his fist. "I'll learn her a lesson or two."

"I knew you didn't have the nerve to face me alone, Black Diamond," smiled Kit.

"Damn you, Bull, take that one-legged old buzzard and get out. I'll take care of this little chippie."

"Well," agreed Bull, "use yor hands on her, not yore tongue." He reluctantly backed out the door, taking the leering Peg Leg with him. Kit quickly shot the bolt on the door. Black Diamond made a move forward. Kit's little gun flashed into sight.

"Lay a hand on that knife of yours and I'll shoot. And if anything should happen to me, there is a friend of mine who will take up my game. Down in New Orleans there's an old indictment for a gal about your size and description. Her name down there is Sue Jackson, Creole Sue. She's still wanted down there for double murder. I though that'd make you squirm. Now behave. And if you give me so much as one small fraction of a lie to the questions I'm going to ask, I'll put you where all your rabbit feet won't do you much good. Listen carefully. Where is Amy Steele?"

"I don't know. So help me God, I don't."

"What do you know about God? Leave His name off your dirty tongue. Where's Amy Steele? The truth is what I'm after. I'm holdin' all the aces, queen. Talk turkey. Where's Amy Steele?"

"I don't know. I don't want to know, you shanty Irish chippie."

"Kindly leave off the compliments, Creole Sue. You've been working your witch gags on Ma Clanton and her old man. You and this Klink thing went down there and put the old hag over the jumps. You got a story out of her about her two un-hung sons and Amy Steele, but you don't dare use it just now, because Klink's scared. It was you that got that half-witted old she-devil to coax back her two sons. Don't dare deny that."

"What if I did get the story out of her?" flashed Black Diamond, her eye alight with triumph, "and what if Klink prints it? It's the truth. And listen to me, you red-headed brat, I'm not blind or dumb. You won't be sorry to see that lily-faced little snob dirtied up. You quit a good job here to grab off Joe Morgan. You can't lie out of that."

"I wouldn't try to, dearie. But we're getting off the subject. Amy Steele has disappeared. Where did Tug and Tim Clanton take her?"

"That's their business, not mine. I don't want to know a thing about it. Amy Steele was two-faced enough to speak to me during the smallpox scare when I was some good to her father. After that, her white nose went higher than ever. I hope she remembers how stuck up she was."

"I see your game, now. You and Klink are clever. You're letting Old Lady Clanton do your dirty work. No, I don't suppose you do know where those two whelps have taken her. But listen, you yellow wench, if one word about that girl goes into Klink's paper, you go back to New Orleans and Klink will swing by his neck from a tree."

Kit unbolted the door suddenly. Bull Mitchell almost fell inside. He had been leaning against the door, trying to listen.

"Come in, Bull. I'm finished with the queen. Did you hear anything much about what we were saying?"

"The damn door was too thick," admitted Bull brazenly.

"Has Doc Steele ever hurt you, Bull?"

"Doc? He's the only one of your damned outfit that's worth two-bits. Doc can come here any time. He knows it. Doc Steele is a white man."

"Damn you, Kit Kavanaugh," snarled Black Diamond. "You shut up or I'll cut your heart out."

"No you won't, dearie, because while you're moving that truck-horse frame of yours, I'll be getting some target practice. Stand back. Bull and I have something to talk over." Kit, still watching the other woman, addressed Bull Mitchell again.

"Black Diamond and Klink have ribbed up the two Clanton thugs to kidnap Amy Steele. She can't deny it, neither can Klink. You know it will kill Doc if anything goes wrong with Amy. I'm asking the only favor I ever asked of you, Bull. I'm asking you to help us. You're a tough egg, Bull, but you're not low-down or yellow. You wouldn't hit Doc Steele below the belt. Will you help us find Doc's kid?"

"You're damn' right I will, Kit. And I'll make—"

"Never mind the rest of it. Get your hat and keep your mouth shut. And, Black Diamond, if you even whisper the name of that girl, you and Klink get yours. Come on, Bull."

Chapter Nineteen

DEAD MAN

IT WAS a grim-lipped, hard-eyed group of silent men who rode away into the night. With them rode Kit Kavanaugh.

"Because," she told Doc, "Amy will need me."

No man had ever seen the genial, white-haired doctor as he was to-night. No one had ever seen a gun in his hands before. Kit kept close beside him. In the lead rode Joe Morgan and Bull Mitchell, their stirrups touching as they pressed their horses to a long trot. Tex Calhoun, Pete Smyth and two engineers from the mines brought up the rear. Silent men riding on a sinister errand.

They halted at the Clanton ranch. A light burned inside the house. Joe Morgan and Bull Mitchell entered without rapping. Those who still sat their horses saw Joe and Bull hesitate on the threshold, then enter, closing the door behind them. All save Doc and Kit now dismounted and surrounded the house and barn. Their orders were to shoot to kill if any of the Clantons opened fire.

Inside the house all was quiet save for a moaning, wailing chant. Now the rumbling voice of Bull Mitchell could be heard.

Joe Morgan and Bull Mitchell had entered, not knowing just what to expect. Hardened as they were, they stood rooted to the spot for a moment, appalled.

Before an open grate fire squatted the Clanton woman, her dirty, stringy white hair veiling her bent face like a filthy curtain of greasy strings. Something that gave off a vile, sweetish, sickening odor, was brewing in a pot that hung from an iron crane. The hag's toothless mouth was chanting some heathenish words. No witch in picture or on the stage could have more truly portrayed the gruesome character.

But it was not alone the woman that made Joe and Bull shudder.

Before her, there on the greasy, dirt hearth, lay the almost naked body of a man, its dead flesh clotted with blood. Mutilated almost beyond recognition, head and arms gone. The bony, claw-like, unwashed hands of the hag worked with cleaver and a butcher knife.

"God," breathed Bull Mitchell, white with nausea. Joe had jerked the hag away from her grisly work. She screamed curses at him, mixing her vile blasphemy with a strange jargon. She came at Joe with the cleaver but he knocked it from her hands with his rifle barrel. She dropped to the floor, whimpering and cursing, her shriveled old body across the mutilated thing on the hearth. The decapitated head rolled from under her grimy black shawl. Its face, horribly real, leered at the two men. It was the face of Bill Clanton, mouth agape, eyes staring.

Suddenly the old hag screamed, lurched sideways, and rolled over. Her two skinny hands gripped the red handle of the butcher knife that was buried in her chest. She was dead.

Joe and Bull searched the rest of the house. It was empty. In one room they found three dead cats hanging by their necks from a rafter. Dried bats and snakes adorned the walls. Crudely drawn pictures of Lucifer were marked on the dirty white plaster. There were other markings, mostly without meaning, others lewd. There was a weird sort of altar made of rocks and bleached cattle bones. On the floor in front of it was a dark, sticky smear. There was a double-bitted ax, foul with blood and hair. Some short lengths of bloody ropes.

"She musta tied Bill up when he was drunk, then drug him here," said Bull hoarsely. "Then she begun workin' on him. I'm no weaklin', Morgan, but if I don't git outa this damned place, I'm gonna be sick."

Carrying lanterns, they went outside into the clean air.

"Nobody there but the old woman and she's crazy as a loon," said Joe quickly, before Bull could say a word. He wanted to spare Doc and Kit that scene of horror. Pete and Tex came from their search of the barn and sheds.

"Nobody there, Joe. Got any suggestions?"

"I have," said Bull. "There's some old limestone caves near my place. Tug and Tim hid out there for a while this spring. They might go there, thinkin' I'd never tell about the caves. A man can't see the mouth of the main cave till he's on top of it. It's just about big enough for a man to crawl into. Then inside is a big room, and a smaller cave off that with a short tunnel between the two. There's a sort of underground creek there. It seeps down into the ground and comes up a mile below there at my well house. Till a few years ago, I always thought it was a spring. Then, huntin' grouse one day, I come up on the caves where the real spring is. With grub, they could live there fer years and nobody the wiser."

"That sounds worth trying," nodded Joe, "but it's a one-man job. Two men at the most. The rest of you wait at our ranch. I'll go there with Bull, to have a look at the caves. If we all go, they'll hear us or see us and maybe get away or kill somebody."

"It's my job, Joe," said Doc.

"Not this time, Doc," Joe told him. "Bull and I will handle this."

"Joe is right," put in Kit. "And quit worrying, Doc. I know Amy is all right. I've never known one of my hunches to go wrong. I just know she's all right," and to herself she silently added, "And may the Lord forgive me for that lie."

Between them, she and Pete Smyth managed to drive away that terrible hopeless look in Doc's eyes.

Joe and Bull Mitchell swung off the main road and took a twisting trail that slanted across the rimrock, down a ridge, and into a long draw that became chocked with buck-brush and choke-cherry thickets. The going was slower here.

"There's something damned queer about this whole business, Mitchell," said Joe Morgan. "Why did the Clanton boys pull out last year? Why did they come back here and kidnap Amy Steele? And who put all those crazy notions in Ma Clanton's head? I'm going to the bottom of this and whoever ribbed this dirty game will hang for it."

"You ain't in office yet, Morgan. Many a drink has bin poured that never went down a man's throat. Meanin', between you and me, that you might git elected but yuh'll never work at the job."

"You can't bluff me, Bull. And if this is a trap to catch me, you're even a bigger blackguard than I figured you. You're into the game somewhere. And I'm watching every move you make. I might kill you, to-night."

"If you're damned lucky, yuh might. So you figger this is just a trap, do yuh? Why didn't yuh fetch along yore friends, then?"

"Because it takes a better man than you to scare me, Mitchell."

"Well, I'll be damned," rumbled Bull in an undertone. Bull admired courage, even in an enemy. And if Joe Morgan suspected this to be a trap, then he was indeed a brave man to take his chances alone.

Suddenly they both reined up sharply. For up ahead, there against a limestone ledge that stood like a giant black table against the starlit sky, showed a glimmer of light. It flickered, then vanished. Some one with a lantern was up there.

"Somebody's up there at the cave, Morgan. And listen, you damned young idiot, this ain't a trap. When the time comes fer me to get yuh, I'll get yuh in the open. Up yonder is the two Clantons. There's two of us. And to show yuh my heart's in the right place, I'll go ahead. If I show snake sign, you get a free shot at my back."

They dismounted and crept on afoot, Bull leading the way.

Despite his bulk, the saloon man made little noise as he negotiated the brush flanked trail. There was only a sliver of moon and its pale light was blotted out in the black shadow of the limestone wall.

Again the light, for the fraction of a minute. Then it was gone once more. Bull and Joe gained the mouth of the cave. At a signal from Bull, they crept through the small opening and into a cave that was black as pitch. The heavy odor of stale tobacco smoke and food hung in the cave, making the blackness seem almost stifling and weirdly, intangibly thick, as if it had substance.

At the far end of the cave showed a faint glimmer. Joe guessed that this was the tunnel entrance leading to the second cave.

Joe reached out his left hand to touch Bull. But Bull was not there. Joe stiffened, his thumb on his gun hammer, his nerves pulled taut. Was it a trap, this black, stifling cave?

The tunnel hole was now blotted out. Joe went forward warily. Some one was crawling through the connecting tunnel, blocking the dim light beyond. Joe stumbled over some bulky object—a kiack box, filled with pans and grub. It upset noisily.

The next instant a dull, ear-jarring roar filled the cave. Another roar, and another. Then an echoing silence. The dim light again revealed the connecting tunnel. Joe dove for it, gun ready, reckless of what might be beyond. A moment later his head and shoulders were in the other cave. A lantern burned on a shelf hewed out of the rock. Bull Mitchell stood there, a smoking gun in his hand. The cave was foul with acrid powder smoke. At Bull Mitchell's feet lay the twitching body of Tug Clanton. Save for the dying man, Bull, and Joe, the cave was empty.

Bull's boot toe indicated the gun in Tug Clanton's right hand. "He opened up on me and I got 'im."

Joe bent over the twitching form. His hands gripped the shoulders of the dying man.

"Where's Amy Steele?" Joe asked hoarsely. But Tug Clanton was dead, his body limp in death, even as the question left Joe's lips.

Bull Mitchell bit the end from a black cigar, pulled the head of a match across the boot sole of the dead man, and the match flame showed the big man's face with its faint grin of triumph. Joe examined the dead man. Three bullet holes in his back. Tug's six-shooter had not been fired. Joe straightened up, facing Bull Mitchell across Tug Clanton's murdered body.

"Dead men don't talk, do they, Mitchell?"

Bull Mitchell rolled Tug's body over with his foot.

"He had it comin'. He got it. When Tim shows up with Doc's girl, we'll be here waitin', instead of Tug."

Bull scowled as Joe went through the dead man's pockets. There was a dangerous light in the saloon man's eyes as he watched the search. But he smiled with one corner of his mouth as Joe's search proved fruitless.

There were two tarp-covered beds in the second cave; also a pile of provisions and empty cans piled in a far corner: signs that told Joe that the two Clantons had made the cave their home for many months. Joe took the lantern and examined some carvings on the limestone walls, cut in the soft rock with pocket knives. He paled a little, and his eyes slitted as he saw Amy's name, linked with Tug's and Tim's, there in a dozen places. Other words, obscene words, were scratched there.

Joe turned away, his face set grimly. Bull Mitchell was startled to note the resemblance of that face to the face of Wade Morgan, the father. Alike in every feature, Bull was on his guard now, his eyes watching the younger man. He was reminded of that day, years ago, when a small boy had squinted along the barrel of a Winchester and snarled at him to stand where he was or he'd be killed. This was the true son of Wade Morgan, killer.

'Mitchell,' rasped Joe, "if I had the remotest idea that you were mixed up in this damned kidnaping, I'd kill you as easy as you killed Tug Clanton. You knew the Clantons were using this cave?"

"Yes. But I didn't know they was plannin' any kidnapin'. Doc Steele always played fair with me. I'd be a skunk and worse if I was party to this dirty business. I don't lay claim to many good points, Morgan, but even a man like me has got his limits. I ain't afraid of you or any other man. It ain't through any fear of you that I say I wasn't mixed up in this deal. Take it or leave it, Joe Morgan."

Joe was forced to believe that Bull Mitchell told the truth. He put up his gun.

"Do you reckon Tim will bring Amy here?" he asked.

"Unless he sets out to double-cross his brother. It's plain that Tug was here waitin'. Look at him, there. Shaved, clean clothes. There's a big box of candy and some perfume in a bottle."

Joe picked up a gaudy imitation Spanish shawl from one of the bunks. Bull's eyes narrowed a little. He recognized that shawl as one that had belonged to Black Diamond. But Joe had no way of connecting the shawl with the queen of Whisky Gulch.

"We'd better wait in the front cave," suggested Bull. "The air is better in there."

"After you," said Joe coldly. They left the lantern burning in the rear cave. There, in the bigger cave, they began their vigil. A match or two had shown the bigger cave to be empty, save for some pack gear, some shotguns and rifles, and a big store of ammunition.

Two hours of waiting. Joe became restless, galled by the inactivity and suspense.

"Doc had ought to know," spoke Bull, also impatient. "One of us could slip down to my place and tell the others our plans."

"I'll wait here," said Joe. Bull hesitated for a long moment, then growled assent. He left Joe there and went back down the steep trail.

Alone, Joe waited there in the darkness, his peace of mind haunted by a thousand disturbing thoughts. The least sound sent his blood pulsing faster. His eyes pained from the constant staring out into the mocking darkness.

Hours dragged past. Out there in the darkness a twig snapped. There came the low murmur of voices. Joe crouched, his gun ready. Then Bull Mitchell's hail shattered Joe's hopes.

"Anybody show up, Morgan?"

"No."

With Bull came Tex Buford and the mining engineer. Pete and Kit had stayed with Doc, who was near the breaking-point from anxiety and grief. The genial doctor who had cheered so many others in their times of sorrow could not lighten his own burden. Mrs. Steele, as yet ignorant of Amy's disappearance, was spared, so far. But it would be only a matter of a few hours until she must share her husband's burden. Kit had sent Joe a sealed note. Tex handed it to him. He crawled back into the lantern-lit cave beyond and read its message.

"Destroy this," read the note, "when you've read it. Have good reason to know that Tim might try to double-cross Tug. Advise leaving Tex there at the cave. He and the mining engineer can stay there with Bull. Come here alone to the ranch. Have a hunch. Hurry."

Chapter Twenty

WARNING!

A MAN met Joe at the barn, there as the Morgan-Burch ranch. At first Joe did not recognize him.

"It's me—Casey. Miss Kit said ta meet ya out here at the barn, see. An' ta let 'er know when ya got here. Her'n Pete Smyth is at da house wit' da Doc. I'll go get 'er. You stay here."

A few moments later Kit returned with Casey. The big, red-faced fighter seemed ill at ease.

"Casey's afraid he might have been followed here," explained Kit. "If they get wise to him, his name is mud. Black Diamond already suspects him. She's been watching him for the past month. But she couldn't prove anything and she knew that Bull wouldn't can Casey without positive proof that Casey was a spy in their dirty camp. Casey, understand, is none other than Pete's mysterious Moccasin Tracks. He and Pete are old pals. And Casey has been all for you since the night you licked Bull. Now tell Joe what you told Pete and me, Casey."

"De Clantons has bin workin' fer Bull Mitchell on de quiet," began Casey in a husky whisper. "Doin' his doity little jobs. Like gettin' some old prospector drunk an' talkin'. I know t'ree claims Bull gets, see, when da prospector kinda disappears. Good claims, see, wort jumpin'. De Clantons slips a shot uh cyanide in de old prospector's drink. Den dey toin his body over to de ol' lady an' she gits rid of it. Doity woik. Dem two Clanton kids does de jobs. Bill Clanton is scairt. He tries to run off, but he cain't. De old lady is clean bughouse wit' dope dat Black Diamond slips 'er as part of de witch gag. Bill's scairt uh de old dame an' I don't blame him. I bet she croaks 'im some day."

"She murdered him not more than twelve hours ago," said Joe. "Bull and I walked in on the old she-devil and she killed herself. Go ahead with the story, Casey."

"Well, Klink blows inta town wit' 'is newspaper gag. Bull ain't wise, see, but Klink an' Black Diamond is old pals. Klink's got somethin' or 'er an' he makes 'er declare him in on her game. Bull don't like dis Klink but he does about what de queen says, see. Sometimes I t'ink he's stuck on 'er.

"Now dis Klink is a slick boid. He sees where he can chisel Bull outa da game. He makes Black Diamond play in wit' 'im. Dey loads Ol' Lady Clanton up wit' hop an' tells her ta rib up her two boys ta pull some kinda job. I can't get what it is, see, but it's somethin' doity. Dey got de ol' lady in a back room an' I hears 'im ribbin' her wit' slick talk an' money ta buy more hop. She okays, see. An' de nex' night Tim Clanton slips inta town an' hides out a Black Diamond's joint.

"I t'ink she's got him on da hop like she gits de ol' dame. Klink an' Black Diamond an' dis Tim boid talks a while. I hear dis Tim Clanton say he's gonna let Tug wait till he grows white whiskers longer'n a horse's tail. Klink tells him ta suit hisself about dat. Dat all dey want is de job done right. Dat's all I hears. When I slip up dere again, Tim's gone. Klink an' Black Diamond is splittin' a quart uh Mum's.

" 'We'll bleed dis boig,' says Klink. 'Dey'll pay twenty t'ousand. Even Bull'll donate fer de reward dough. It's a pipe. We'll split de twenty grand two ways, let dis Tim sap take de raps, an' I'll spend me old age in Buenos Aires, livin' like a dook.'

" 'Wit Black Diamond right by yore side,' puts in de queen. An' later on de two of 'em goes back into de saloon, innercent as two boids.

"But I'm still dumb, see, because I don't get hep to deir doity woiks. It's after Miss Kit comes in last evenin' an' after readin' Black Diamonds de rules, beats it wit' Bull, dat I git wise. Black Diamond goes screwy, see. Raises hell around, beatin' up a couple dames an' bawlin' out customers an' tellin' Klink he's a lousy bum. Klink coaxes 'er into de printin' office an' tells me ta mix up a stiff one wit' plenty absinthe in it, and make it two while I'm at it. I listens outside de door a minute. De queen says she's gonna croak Miss Kit an' Pete Smyth. She says Bull will twist 'er neck off when he gits back. Her an' Klink is bot' scairt about somethin', an' I hears 'em say somethin' about a reward note.

"Den I brings in de drinks. Stiff, like Klink orders, wit' plenty absinthe. It ain't fifteen minutes later I answer de buzzer from deir printin' shop. Dey're in a swell humor now. De woild is deir setup, see, an' dey're gonna kayo it fer de big count. Klink an' her has pencils an' paper.

" 'Set dem drinks down,' Klink yaps at me, 'an' get ta hell outa here.'

"Dago comes on shift about den an' I skins off me apron an' gits me coat. Den I takes a walk aroun' in de park. I sees Klink slip somethin' in under Joe Morgan's door. When he goes back, an' de track's clear, I gits de letter he slips inta Joe's office. Read it." Casey thrust a soiled square of cheap paper into Joe's hand and held a match for light. The wording was crudely printed, obviously disguised.

WARNING!

If you want your Amy back, rustle $20,000 and have it in unmarked cash. Leave it under big white rock known as Jackson's rock on river road. Every move you make will be watched, so come alone and don't try any tricks. Put money under white rock at exactly noon. Ride away slow. Take trail leading to old outlaw cabin on Crooked Creek. Wait there. Your Amy will meet you there. At first sign of trickery on your part, Amy Steele dies. I mean business.

AN ENEMY.

"The devils!" croaked Joe huskily. "By God, I'll—"

"You'll do exactly as the note demands, Joe," said Kit. "Tim Clanton has Amy hidden somewhere near that cabin on Crooked Creek. You can bet your last peso that Klink and the queen aren't declaring Tim in on the money. He's probably expecting the money to be left at the cabin, instead of at Jackson's rock, up at the head of the breaks. So your best bet, in order to keep Amy from harm, is to do exactly as the queen wants. Rustle the money. Do it quietly, but in such a manner that Klink and the queen will know it. Tex and Bull and the mines will have that much. Take the money to the rock. Leave it there and ride down to the cabin. Bull will handle Black Diamond and Klink, never fear. And I'll be taking care of Amy."

"What do you mean, Kit, taking care of Amy?" asked Joe.

"Well," said Kit, "there's some sort of an old adage about the plans of mice and men often going haywire. I've a notion that Tim Clanton has unwittingly played into our hands, if he planned on making use of the cabin on Crooked Creek. Because that's where Wade Morgan is waiting for Long Bob and Almanac, who plan to make a two-day circle, thus throwing Patchen and his men off the scent. Almanac and Long Bob planned to cross the river, come up the south side, cross over at night, and meet Wade at the cabin. That brings them there some time to-morrow night. Meanwhile, Wade is at the cabin and it's Tim Clanton's tough luck if he shows his ugly face there. I shouldn't wonder but what Wade Morgan and Amy are there, safe as if they were in jail. So don't worry about Amy, Joe. I'll take care of her. I plan to start right away for the cabin on Crooked Creek."

"But you don't know where it is, Kit."

"But I do, Joe. Almanac took me there the first time. The second and third times I went there I rode alone and at night. Wade and I used it for a post-office."

"The devil!"

"Exactly, Joe. Now you lope on back to town, pretend to find that note, and put on your act. We'll catch Black Diamond and Ambrose Klink in their own putrid trap."

"Gosh, Kit," exclaimed Joe, "you're the—"

"The darndest chump that ever lived," finished Kit, as she led her horse from the barn and swung into the saddle. "And I don't need to warn you to be well heeled on that visit to Jackson's rock, Joe. You might have to kill brother Klink." She gave her horse a free rein and was gone in the night.

Over inside the house, Pete Smyth was doing his best to cheer up Doc Steele.

"Just leave it to Kit, Doc. She's the best little miracle worker this side of Paradise, even if she does use marked cards to get results. Chip off the old Kavanaugh block. The Deacon was the same way. He'd gamble on anything and usually won. The luck of the Irish, he said it was, but mostly it was his nerve and wit and underneath it, a brain that was the brain of a genius. Kit'll win for you and Amy. Sure she will. Kit's the grandest girl in the world, Doc."

Chapter Twenty-one

LITTLE KIT

WADE MORGAN ejected an empty shell from his six-shooter. The dark cabin reeked with powder fumes. The heavy body in the open doorway twitched and became quiet. Wade struck a match and held it close to the dead man's face. "Damned if it ain't one of Bill Clanton's whelps." The match went out. The last echoes of Wade's gun faded in the silence of the box cañon.

Tim Clanton had left Amy, tied in her saddle, a short distance away. He had gone on to the cabin on foot to investigate. As he opened the door a low challenge came out of the black interior:

"Who's there?"

Tim had given reply to the challenge with quick gunfire. Bullets had thudded into the log wall behind Wade. Then Wade's trigger finger perked and Tim Clanton, last of his inbred clan, had slumped down, to die with his boots on and a smoking gun in his hand.

"Any fool had ought to know," mused Wade, as he pulled on his boots, "that when he stands in a doorway he's makin' a good target outa—"

From down the cañon a woman's thin cry of terror broke into the outlaw's musings. He stepped across Tim's hulking body and ran toward the sound, swearing softly under his breath. A moment later he was telling the terrified Amy Steele that everything was all right. That there was nothing to be so scared about. In the dim light she stared at this thin-featured man with white hair and mustache, who held a naked gun in his hand as his knife cut her free from the restless horse.

"Would you mind, lady, tellin' me who yuh are and how come yo're here?" For it had been many years since Wade Morgan had seen Amy Steele.

"My name is Amy Steele. Tim Clanton brought me here. Whoever you are, you've saved my life. I had planned on killing myself tonight. Since Tim and Tug Clanton kidnaped me once before, I've always feared a repetition and carried a little vial of poison. Where is Tim?"

"Dead." Wade lifted her from the saddle. The effort made him cough weakly. "So this is little Amy, done growed up," he said, in that weak, toneless voice that seemed to lack sufficient strength to carry any inflection. "I don't reckon you'd recollect me, much. I'm Joe Morgan's Dad."

"I remember," said Amy, shocked at his wasted appearance.

He looked like a feeble old man past seventy, save for the quick-moving hands and eyes that glittered under thick, bushy brows. Eyes that were slits of fire that shone through the gray ashes of a burned-out fire. A queer expression, meant to be a smile, crossed his thin face. He understood the mingled horror and pity and fear of him that made her tremble as he took her arm to guide her along the dim trail. He had just killed a man. And although that man was more beast than human, Amy Steele thought of him as a living being whos life's candle had been snuffed out by Wade Morgan's gun. Amy was angry with herself for being too sensitive.

"Better wait here, Amy." Wade left her there in the trail. She heard him slowly dragging some heavy thing into the brush near the cabin. Heard him breathing heavily from the exertion. After some minutes he returned to her and led the way to the cabin.

"It won't do to light a light," he told her. "On account of that fool posse of Sim Patchen's that's sashayin' around. Sound carries a long ways. Like as not they heard the shootin'. Come mornin', we'll see about gettin' yuh home, Amy. This shack ain't really fixed fer female company, but I reckon you kin make out. Hungry?"

"I feel right now like I never wanted another bite," she said, trying to calm her shattered nerves.

"I'll fix yuh up some whisky an' water. It'll kind quiet yuh. Then you kin lay down and rest. How's Doc and yore maw?" He was mixing the toddy. Accustomed as he was to the lack of light, he moved about as well as if the dark cabin were lighted. He kept on talking in a matter-of-fact tone. Her visit there might have been a most casual one. Nor did Wade Morgan let her know that the shot that had saved her life had, by its echoes, damned his chances of ever leaving this cabin alive. Sim Patchen and his men would be closing in on him. Pete Smyth and Kit Kavanaugh would have made their plea to the governor in vain.

It was getting daylight. Dawn was chasing the darkness out of the cañon. Instinct, the same sort of instinct given to hunted thing, told Wade Morgan that the posse would be guarding the trail that led out. He got a grim sort of satisfaction from knowing that no man among them dared come near the cabin by daylight. They would probably wait for the black protection of another night before their dread circle closed in on the cabin. Before their guns blazed, bullets rattling like giant hail against the log walls.

He was astonished when, from a safe distance, a voice hailed the cabin, Sim Patchen's voice.

"Halloooo! Halloooo, there at the cabin!"

Wade Morgan barred the door and Winchester in hand, turned to Amy. "Better lay flat under the bunk in case it's a trick." His voice was brittle. Then he gave reply to Patchen's hail.

"What's eatin' on yuh, Patchen?"

"That you, Wade Morgan?"

"No, it's my grandmother. What's on yore mind?"

"Is Amy Steele there?"

"She is. Safe and sound as a new dollar. Is Doc there tuh take her?"

"No. Kit Kavanaugh. She come to fetch Amy Steele back home. We picked her up durin' the night, just afore daylight. Where's Tim Clanton?"

"He hired out on a job kickin' hot clods at a place called Hell. Send Kit Kavanaugh here to the cabin. Amy kin go back with her. No tricks, Patchen."

"Don't you try any tricks, Wade Morgan!"

"You ain't got any brighter since we last met, Sim," called Wade. "I ain't riskin' the lives of these two girls with any fool tricks. You mighta made a shore success as a dog ketcher, Sim, because that's the sort of brains yuh got. Send over Kit Kavanaugh."

There was a short wait; then Kit rode across the clearing. She dismounted and stepped to the door. Wade admitted her.

"A sight fer any man's eyes, as yuh come ridin' acrost there," said Wade. His face had lost its grim lines. He took her hand with a smile, as Kit closed the door.

Amy came forward, her face a little flushed. The two women looked at one another; then Kit laughed shakily and took Amy in her arms. "Have a swell cry, honey," said Kit, holding the other girl tightly.

"I . . . I just can't hate you," came in muffled tones from Amy's buried face. "You . . . you're. . . ."

"Everything's all right, kid. Only don't let this kidnaping gag get to be a habit. Supposing it had rained or something and me without a slicker, gadding around losing my beauty sleep, eating

113

ham and beans with Sim Patchen, and handing the big dunce a line of corral dust that was simply scandalous. I ran slap-dab into 'em in the dark. Scared me silly. Says I to myself, 'Kit, you're the biggest chump since Brody did his high dive.' Then Sim Patchen up and tells me that I'm a prisoner of war or something. He's heard shots up in the neighborhood and is about to pull a raid. Then I explains that I'm hunting a lady that was lost and I make him see the light. The way I played up to that bum's vanity was a sin. And here I am." Kit gently pushed Amy into a homemade chair and faced Wade.

"Pete and I put it over at Helena, Wade. Bob and Almanac will get here some time to-night with a warrant for your arrest. It's all hunky-dory. Too bad Patchen had to get tipped off that you were here. But that's spilled milk. We'll out-fox that dumb cop yet." Kit turned back to Amy, who had regained her composure and was listening intently.

"Amy," said Kit firmly, "you're about to bust the law by aiding a fugitive. My horse is outside. In about five minutes you're going out and you're going to get on him and ride him like you owned him, once you get well past the posse. Instead of taking the north fork of the road that leads to Pay Dirt, swing south. You know where the old bull-whacker road crosses the river. Well, stop there. Go out on the sand bar and make a driftwood fire. Put some green willows on it to make a lot of smoke. If you have a gun, shoot a few times. And when Bob Burch or Almanac show up on the other bank, tell them to come on across. When they get on this side, tell 'em to ride like the devil was after 'em. I'll help Wade hold back Patchen's gang till they get here."

Wade Morgan looked at Kit, his hazel eyes warm with admiration. Then he slowly shook his white head.

"Yo're game, and it's shore white of you. But I'd heap rather hang than have any woman do my fightin' fer me. You two girls get ready an' pull out. Don't worry, Kit, I'll be right here when Bob an' Alamanac git here. I still have a good fight left in my system an' Patchen is not fool enough tuh take chances with Wade Morgan. Better be draggin' it. Sim's hollerin' out yonder. A-bawlin' like a lost yearlin'."

When Amy Steele tried to thank him again, Wade cut her off gruffly. "Give my best to Doc an' yore mother, Amy."

"I'm getting word to Long Bob," said Kit, as she took his hand in both hers. "They'll get here this afternoon. So will Joe. So-long, Wade." Kit tried to keep her voice cheerful and matter-of-fact. She knew Wade's fear of sentiment. Even as she knew that this was their last farewell.

"So-long, Kit Kavanaugh. Take care uh that Pete feller, and keep an eye on Joe. You've bin a real pardner."

Kit, leading her horse, walked back across the clearing, Amy with her. At the edge of the clearing, Kit paused and turned. She waved a farewell, and saw Wade Morgan's hat wave from the window. And so a friendship, a comradeship strange in its making, fierce in its loyalty, made its last gallant gesture.

Chapter Twenty-two

DOUBLE CROSS

DOC STEELE, Pete Smyth, and Joe Morgan were back in Pay Dirt. Casey was back behind his bar. Bull Mitchell had returned and now sat in his office, his red eyes fixed on Black Diamond, who sat in a chair, ugly and sullen under Bull's cross-questioning.

Bull called Casey.

"If Joe Morgan comes in, give him this package. There is ten thousand buck in the package, so don't handle it careless. Where in hell is Klink?"

"Dunno, Bull. I went off shift at eight last night. Dago was on. I had a date, see, wit' a dame, an' I didn't hang aroun' de joint."

"Date, huh?" sneered Black Diamond, "with some broad, huh? What's the skirt's name, Casey?"

"A guy that squeals on a lady is a bum," grinned Casey.

"Yeh?" The queen's voice became harder. "How about a stool pigeon, Casey? He ain't a bum, huh? Roll that up with the next pill you cook."

"What are you gettin' at?" Bull growled at her. "Have ya gone loco or are yuh drunk again?"

"Me?" Black Diamond laughed mirthlessly. "I'm loco, all right, just like a fox. This big louse works for Pete Smyth. Tell me I lie, if you think you can get away with it, Mr. Moccasin Tracks."

"What's she talkin' about, Casey?" growled Bull.

"She says I'm a friend of Pete Smyth's and Joe Morgan's. And she didn't lie when she said it."

"The hell ya say? Been double-crossin' me, have ya, Casey?"

Casey faced his boss with a fearless grin.

"Keep yore shirt tail from gettin' in a knot, Bull. Ya licked me once, an' ya might do it gain. But I ain't afraid an' you know it. Me'n Pete Smyth is old-time friends, see. An' I kinda like dis Joe Morgan kid, see. But I never done you no poisonal doit. What I done, I done because I ain't lettin' de queen here turn de hooks into Kit Kavanaugh who is a square gal an' a lady. If ya wanta take dat outa me hide, Bull, I'll go as far I can wit' ya." Casey untied his bar apron and spat on his hands.

"Put on yore apron, Casey. I'll settle your bill later. When Joe Morgan comes in, give him that dough. Never mind what it's for. And when Klink shows up, send him in here. Now get ta hell out a here and take care of the trade."

Alone again with Black Diamond, Bull bit the end off a big black cigar, pulled a match head across the sole of the queen's French-heeled slipper, and watched her obliquely. He knew her, knew how silence on his part would do more than any questioning. As yet unaware of the extent of Black Diamond's duplicity, Bull was merely playing his gambler's hunch that she and Klink were playing some crooked game. He was simply letting her own conscience goad her into speaking. His bloodshot eyes never left her face.

"Well," she finally snarled, "what are you going to do about it? Don't forget what I have on you. You and the Clantons. Don't try anything you can't finish. You and your red-headed chippie. She's got you playing monkey on a stick."

"Leave Kit outa this." He blew a cloud of smoke in her face, and lapsed into another silence.

They heard Joe Morgan come in. Heard Joe and Casey talk a moment, their words blurred by the partition that separated the bar from Bull's private office. Then Joe went outside and mounted his horse. Black Diamond instinctively looked at her watch. Ten-forty. Just time enough, by steady riding, to make Jackson's rock. She pulled the drawn shade aside and peeped out, just as Joe rode away.

"What made you give Joe Morgan ten thousand bucks, you big fool?"

"Paying off another of your damned fool debts. You're mixed up in that kidnaping. Sit down." He again summoned Casey.

"I'm goin' for a walk, Casey," he informed the big bartender. "The queen is gonna stay here to hold down the office. If she tries ta get out, knock her stiff. If Klink shows up, hold 'im."

Black Diamond went a little white under her paint. She bit her red lip until a thread of blood showed on her powdered chin. Her eyes seemed to contract and become black beads of light. One jeweled hand was inside the low cut bosom of her red satin dress, its fingers wrapped around her long-bladed knife. Bull leered at her, put on his hat, and buckling on a heavy cartridge belt, transferred his gun from the waistband of his checked trousers to a carved leather holster. Without another word, he let himself out the door. Casey went with him.

Black Diamond watched Bull go up the street and turn up a trail that led to Klink's cabin. She smiled heavily and heaved a sigh of relief. Because she knew that Ambrose Klink was not at his cabin—that the blackmailer-editor was waiting at a certain spot along the road, not far from Jackson's rock. Klink, his brain afire with absinthe and drugs, was waiting for the coming of Joe Morgan, planning to kill Joe as he rode past.

After that bit of murder Klink would keep on going. He and Black Diamond would meet in New York. No, Klink would not be at his cabin. Not any more, ever. His last gift to Pay Dirt, the final edition of the *Six-Shooter*, a hundred copies all told, was in the keeping of Black Diamond, well hidden. Together they had got out that edition. It contained a number of interesting and very damning items concerning the past activities of Bull Mitchell. Enough to put that gentleman of parts behind prison bars for the remainder of his life. It played up the abduction of Amy Steele, terming it a sordid love pact between the doctor's daughter and the two Clanton boys. It was as clever a bit of filth as ever had come from the agile brain of Ambrose Klink. Another item condemned Kit Kavanaugh in no uncertain terms. And as a parting shot at Bull Mitchell, it gave a statement of ownership, thus laying the saloon man open to all sorts of libel suits.

Bull Mitchell, once out of sight of the saloon, made a circle that led him to Black Diamond's private cabin in Whisky Gulch. Bull broke the lock with a heave of his heavy shoulder and went inside. Without ceremony he broke open the locks of two trunks. His big hands dove into the trunks, disgorging their contents. A pile of old dresses, some quilts, cheap finery, odds and ends. Useless, worthless trash. Junk. Not a trace of her wealth of gowns and wraps and furs, given her by Bull. The queen had somehow smuggled all her valuable things out, leaving only a couple of trunks filled with trash. The closet and dresser drawers held but a few tawdry rags.

In the middle of the littered floor stood big Bull Mitchell. His cold anger had left him. His heavy-jawed head shook slowly sidewise, as if he could not believe what his eyes saw. In his own peculiar way, he had loved Black Diamond. He had given to her with both hands, given lavishly, after the manner of his kind with their women. He had shared his secrets with her. Black Diamond had become part of his life. Even when he was unfaithful to her, he still cared for her and was proud of her because she ran out the other women who threatened to steal him from her. His inability to hold her had never entered his mind. But it was more than his pride that was hurt now as he read the signs of her change. He left the place with heavy steps, head sagged forward, his eyes dull with pain. He went back to his saloon, entering by way of its back door.

Save for a sleeping bar bum, there on the pool table, the saloon was empty. Casey was not behind the bar. Bull strode along the bar and shoved open the office door. Sprawled on the floor lay Casey, the pearl hilt of Black Diamond's knife protruding from his back. There was no trace of the queen of Whisky Gulch.

Moccasin Tracks had been paid off in full.

Chapter Twenty-three

SIX-GUN TRAIL

NOT a cloud broke the blue of the sky above Joe Morgan as he rode along the trail. A meadowlark sang its liquid-noted song. A covey of sage hens winged across the trail and dropped into a Coulée. Cattle grazed on the hills. The air was softly invigorating, pure and clean, and filled with the sun and the scent of sage. Truly, it was a morning meant to be given over to peaceful things.

Joe looked at his watch. It was a few minutes past eleven o'clock. Ahead, the trail swung off into some broken hills. Tall cottonwood trees and box elder trees showed their green tops above the ridge, marking the path of a creek. This was the head of Jackson Creek. Five miles beyond where the trail crossed the creek, was the big white boulder known as Jackson's rock. Down along the creek were the sagging walls of the old Jackson ranch, deserted these past ten years and longer. Some said that the place was haunted. It had been used as a burying ground, in the early days, when the Indians claimed that section of the land. It had been the scene of sun dances, torture stakes, and medicine lodges. The Sioux had massacred the Jackson family there. A scouting party from the old Seventh Cavalry had there attacked the Sioux and killed a number of them. Grass covered the old graves of white men and Indians. It had been used as a stage station and some gun fights had settled forever the grudges of river bad-men.

Up on the ridge were buffalo bones and round circles of rocks that had once held down the tepees of the Indians camped there.

Down among the cottonwoods and box elder trees, now covered by the hand of nature with rose bushes and service berry bushes, were the graves of the white men who had died there. For all its beauty, its stillness, its green foliage and silver water, the Jackson place still retained its air of mystery and death. Its quiet was the stillness of the grave, even the songs of birds seemed hushed.

Since his boyhood, the place had always intrigued Joe Morgan. He had always experienced the boy's shivering, deliciously hair-raising thrill of mystery as he rode off the ridge into the shadows of those tall cottonwoods that had been there, silent watchers of bloodshed and horror. Even as he had grown older, he had retained, in a measure, that same sensation of nameless fear as he rode along the trail. The hair along the back of his neck always seemed to stiffen as he dropped from the sunwashed ridge into the cool green shadows below.

To-day, traveling on a mission that was grim and dangerous, Joe Morgan felt all that old childhood sensation of dread and expectancy as he let his horse swing down off the ridge. Other men had ridden down, even as he now rode, to fill a grave below. If a man's enemies planned ambush, this was the ideal spot for murder. The thick brush below might hide a score of men, unseen, watching.

He had reached the foot of the slope now, and rode along a grass-filled trail that wound its way through the trees and brush. Joe felt an almost uncontrollable urge to whistle, as a small boy tries to whistle away fear. His raw nerves were playing tricks on him, he told himself. He needed a good sleep and some warm food and . . . A horse nickered loudly.

Joe Morgan quit his horse with a sidewise leap, his right hand reaching for his gun. A rifle bullet chipped the horn of the saddle he had just left. Joe was crashing through the thick brush now. Something moved ahead there, beyond those red willows. Joe's .45 ripped loose its waiting slugs. His second shot brought a thin, screaming curse from Klink, who was running away, firing wildly over his shoulder. Joe caught a swift glimpse of the crouched, running man. He shot again. Klink went down, his lanky form threshing about in the brush, his nasal, terror-racked voice calling for mercy.

"I'm hurt! I'm hurt! Don't shoot again, Morgan! God, I'm dying!" Joe ran up to him, kicked the man's gun from his hand and made a quick examination. Klink was hit in the shoulder and hip. Neither wound was very dangerous if the blood was checked and infection did not set in.

"Of course, Klink, you'll bleed to death if I don't patch you up. So if you don't want to die a slow death you'll answer my questions."

"Don't let a man die, Morgan!" pleaded Klink. "So help me, I'll tell you anything you want to know! Only don't let me die!"

As Joe Morgan bandaged the man's wounds, Klink talked. When he had finished his sordid tale of treachery and blackmail and intended murder, Joe tied him to a tree and left him.

"Mind, Klink, if you wiggle much, those bandages will slip and you'll be several hours dying. Lie quietly, like the yellow, mangy cur you are, and you'll live many a long year in the penitentiary."

And Joe rode away from the whining, whimpering, begging Klink.

Chapter Twenty-four

THE GREAT DIVIDE

PERHAPS, even had fate granted Wade Morgan, outlaw, the privilege of choosing the manner of his passing from life, he would not have changed what was now given him. Here, alone, in this log cabin that had given shelter to so many others of his kind, he waited, unafraid, for the end. This was the end of his trail, the last stand that he would ever make against the law. Broken in health, with only days of suffering and emptiness ahead, death was far better.

There, outside, the sun was lowering in its azure sky. Wild roses bloomed. Birds sang. This was marked on his book as the last day, his last sunset, his last lingering twilight when the songs of the birds were hushed and only the whispering of the pines, like nuns at prayer, crept into the silence and became part of it.

Patchen and his men lay in wait, out there beyond the brush thickets, for the coming of darkness. Now and then a bullet would thud into the door, the crack of the rifle startling the birds into silence. Wade Morgan watched the clearing, smoking, watching the lengthening shadows.

Sometimes he smiled to himself, the hard light gone from his eyes. He thought of his boyhood, perhaps, those years of carefree cowpuncher life. The long, dusty days of the trail herds, comradeships, dances in town, the snow-bound line camps. Of Almanac, whose real name Wade had never known, whose tales had filled his boyhood. Of Hattie, who had run away with him and helped him make the only home he had ever known. Those days when he and Long Bob had dug post holes and built cabins and put in alfalfa. The night Joe was born. Doc Steele, cheerful, sleeves rolled back from white, skillful hands. Bob's soft-spoken words of encouragement. Almanac, his blue eyes misty with the suffering he felt for the little mother, helping Doc, there in the bedroom. . . . Little Britches, with his stick-horse and air-gun. . . . Peaceful days spent in the saddle or at the ranch. Other days and nights when his restless heart ached with that strange urge to leave it all behind and ride out in search of adventure. Almanac's wise eyes watching him, understanding why. . . . Shotgun Riley. . . . The Wild Bunch. The outlaw trail acallin'. Campfires under the stars. Songs of men. The smell of powder smoke and the thrilling grip of excitement when guns cracked and a man was either a coward or a fighter. Friends who would die for a man. . . . Yuma. Where the law took a man's heart and twisted it dry of hope.

A rifle cracked. Wade laughed as he rolled another cigarette. He was glad that Kit was wrong about getting Bob and Almanac here in time. It'd be dark by then. The sun would be down. His last sunset. Wade Morgan would be across the Last Divide.

Wade Morgan could have killed Sim Patchen that afternoon. Sim had shown himself twice. Wade's sights had lined, but he had shot high both times. He wondered why he hadn't killed Patchen. They'd been bad enemies, always.

Kit had said something about Joe coming. He didn't want Joe here. "Hey, there, Patchen!" he called.

"What yuh want, Wade? Gonna surrender?"

"Surrender, hell! If Joe Morgan shows up, corral 'im and hogtie 'im. Don't let him come tuh the cabin."

"Already done it." Sim Patchen's voice was light with triumph. "He put up a hell of a scrap, but he went tuh sleep when a gun barrel got bent acrost his head. He's tied up good, now, tryin' tuh tell me that Bob Burch is a United States marshal an' you agreed tuh surrender tuh Bob."

"He must be outa his head, Patchen."

The sun was almost gone now. It dropped behind the ragged skyline, leaving a red glow behind it. Wade Morgan pinched out the coal of his cigarette and opened the door. A six-shooter in each hand, he stepped out into the open. With an easy, twisting movement he "rolled" both guns, their shots rattling with the speed of an automatic. Puffs of white smoke spotted the brush in a score of places. Wade Morgan, standing with widespread legs, swayed a little. Then he went down, a smile on his lean, tanned face, his eyes looking into the red glow of the setting sun. He was dead, even as he sank slowly to the ground, an empty, smoking gun in each hand.

Wade Morgan had crossed his Last Divide. His last twelve shots had bitten a ragged hole in the trunk of a giant cottonwood. His guns were empty.

Long Bob and Almanac found Joe Morgan there with the body of his father.

The boy's voice was unsteady as he told them how Wade had died.

"There was something terribly splendid about it. I could see his white teeth as he stood there emptying his guns into that big tree, with twenty men shooting at him. He was grinning."

"He died," said Almanac, "like he always said he wanted tuh die. Out in the open, with his face to his last enemies and a gun in his hand. It's all he asked fer. His request was granted."

"The coroner was with the posse," Joe told them. "So they're all through with the body."

They found a rusty shovel and dug a grave, there at the foot of the giant cotton wood. No epitaph could have been more fitting, carved in the finest marble, than those twelve bullets buried there, within the radius of a man's two spread hands, in the trunk of the big tree.

They buried him there, his only coffin a blanket and a trailworn tarp, his head pillowed on his saddle. The three men who had known him best. Kings and men of millions have had fewer friends at their grave. Wade Morgan, outlaw, had asked for little. God seemed to have shown him mercy, there at the end. The sun in his face . . . a quick, brave death, and the hands of friends to lay his body in its grave.

A man of courage had crossed the Big Divide.

Bull Mitchell locked the door of his office. Inside lay the body of Casey. The diamond was gone from Casey's hand. His pockets were empty. The door of the safe was open. Bull also emptied the cash register of its money into the canvas bag he carried.

Peg Leg Love hobbled in. Bull took off his coat and put on one of Casey's spotless aprons. He set out a bottle and two glasses.

Peg Leg, never a talkative sort, said nothing. They touched glasses and drank in silence.

"What time is it, Peg Leg?"

"A little past noon."

"Go on up to the Gulch. Tell all the girls, everybody up there, tuh come on down, after they've packed their stuff and got their trunks out. I'll send the dray up later on, to lug their stuff to the stage office. Round every damn one of 'em up. Tell 'em I'm payin' off."

"You mean that you are—"

"Payin' off." Bull Mitchell selected a cigar from a filled box and lit it. "Rattle that timber leg."

The inhabitants of Whisky Gulch obeyed the summons of their chief. Trunks and bags stood in the wide trail that passed along in front of the log cabins whose shades were always tightly drawn. They seemed to blink a little as they grouped there in the sunlight—like animals driven from their holes into the unaccustomed dayilght. Their unnatural laughter. The harsh lines about their eyes and mouths. Rouge that stood out glaringly against pale skin. Red mouths that tried to smile but had forgotten how. French-heeled slippers and gauze stockings powdered with yellow dust. Imitation jewels that lost their glitter in the revealing light of day.

They seemed strangely timid, grouped there, sitting on trunks and suitcases. A few were openly brazen. They wondered what had happened.

The men, gamblers, parasites, talked in subdued tones. Their poker faces revealed nothing. The professor, a worn, bulging music roll under one arm, sniffed a pinch of white powder, brushed a speck of lint from his blue serge coat, and lit a cigarette. Night birds, routed from their dark roost. One girl with bleached hair was weeping.

"What's the matter, dearie?" asked an older woman.

"I'm damned if I know."

"Fer God's sake let's go down and get a drink."

Lugging bags and suitcases, leaving their trunks there in the trail, they went down the Gulch and into the rear door of the Shotgun Riley saloon. Bull Mitchell greeted them with a one-sided grin. He lined them up and paid them off, one at a time. To each girl he gave a twenty-dollar gold piece. Then he began setting out glasses and bottles. The professor pulled the black cover from the piano and sat down on the rickety stool, a tall white drink at his elbow.

"What'll it be, boss?"

"Give us 'The Blue Bells of Scotland,' professor." That was Bull's favorite song.

Time must have been when the cocaine-sniffing professor had been something besides a honkey-tonk piano thumper. He proved it now as his long yellow fingers strayed with a light touch across the keys.

Bull stood there, listening, his drink untouched. A hush fell across the bar-room. Tears dimmed the hardness of women's eyes. An immaculate tin-horn quit polishing his nails and stared hard at nothing.

The music stopped. Drinks were gulped down throats that ached.

The professor sipped his drink and began playing a popular rag.

Not one of them had asked where Black Diamond was. Bull knew that their eyes had seen long ago, what he had never let himself see.

Throughout the afternoon the drinks came fast. The place was filled with the din of merrymaking. Bull set out more bottles. Empty ones filled the corners and littered the alleyway behind the place. The cash register yawned open, its drawers empty. No money crossed the bar. For it was Bull Mitchell's last pay-off.

Twilight became night. The revelers lost all track of time. For them tomorrow did not exist. Nobody noticed Bull Mitchell's absence.

Pete Smyth, sitting on the veranda of Kit Kavanaugh's cabin, saw a dull red glow, up there in Whisky Culch. A tall, red flame licked the black sky like a dragon's tongue. By the time Pete had reached his office, the Shotgun Riley saloon was afire.

A man came from behind a building. A low-pitched, rumbling voice greeted the newspaper man.

"Damned if I know why, exactly, but I wanted to tell you so-long, Smyth."

Bull Mitchell held out a big, hairy paw.

"Where are you bound for, Bull?"

"Hard tuh say. Take good care of Kit Kavanaugh. . . . And good luck to yuh both. So-long."

"So-long, Bull. Good luck."

He watched the big man mount his dun horse and ride slowly down the street.

Like rats quitting a doomed ship, the men and women of Whisky Gulch spewed from the saloon and stood at the edge of the red glow, watching the old log buildings burn.

Pete passed among them, hunting Casey. No one had seen the big bartender. Pete rushed inside, tried the office door, found it locked.

With a heavy chair he broke down the door. The glow of the fire showed the dead man, there on the floor, the pearl hilt of the knife gleaming from his shoulder blades. Pete backed out, closing the door behind him.

In the back room that had been the office of the *Six-Shooter*, the hot flames licked hungrily at the hidden stack of its last edition.

Klink's last effort had been lost. His swan song had gone unheard.

Ambrose Klink. Sim Patchen, following Joe Morgan's instructions, had found him there at the Jackson place. No ropes bound Klink. There was a gun in his hand . . . and a bullet hole between his eyes. . . . In the soft, wet sand along the creek might have been seen a pair of tracks. A woman's tracks. A woman who wore French-heeled slippers. Beside it, the boot tracks of a large man. Beyond that spot, the sign of two horses, traveling away. . . . A bit of torn paper crushed in the ground under a shod hoof. A bit of it showing. A fragment of penciled words. . . .

$20,000, and have it in unmarked cash. Leave it under big white rock known as Jackson's Rock on river road. . . .

It had been in Casey's pocket when Bull Mitchell searched the bartender's dead body.

Black Diamond and Bull Mitchell were never again heard of in Pay Dirt. The boss of Pay Dirt and his queen had abdicated.

Chapter Twenty-five

AT SUNRISE

SO LAW came to Pay Dirt. On the night that Joe Morgan and Bob Burch were elected, men unbuckled their gunbelts and hung them up to gather dust. Tex Buford and his tin-pan band paraded the streets. Up at the schoolhouse the fiddle squeaked and the accordian moaned. The caller shouted his "balance all" until his voice was hoarse as a cow's.

Joe Morgan and his flushed, happy bride of a few hours, led the grand march. Doc Steele and Almanac were masters of ceremony. Pete Smyth made a grand speech and toasted the bride with pure mountain water.

The simple wedding had been at Kit Kavanaugh's house. Kit, radiant and beautiful as some rare flower, was never more charming nor more bewildering. Even Pete would catch himself staring at her beauty, breathless. He wondered what heartaches were hidden beneath her wit and her golden sheen of beauty. He knew Kit as no one there or anywhere had ever known her. He knew that she was actress enough to hide her hurt. And he wished, with all his heart, that he could make her happy.

He wondered, and felt a little hurt, when she seemed to avoid being alone with him.

They were waltzing together. Pete, worried about her, was silent. "Poor Pete," Kit said softly. "It won't be much longer. To-morrow will come, Pete, and we'll say good-by to Pay Dirt. And don't look so glum, dear. I won't hold you to that promise. You need not marry me, Pete. You've been mighty loyal and splendid and the best pal in the world, dear. I'll never, never forget. And when you're editor of *The World*, I'll—"

"Don't, Kit, please."

The music stopped and Kit was immediately surrounded by a dozen men asking for the next dance. Pete was alone, there at the edge of the crowd. Almanac, a drink in his left hand, plowed his way through the crowd and gripped Pete's hand.

The old fellow's voice was tearful.

"Hell, Pete, I shore hate tuh see yuh goin' away. I was jest a-gittin' the hang uh the dang newspaper layout. Plumb spoilt me fer ranch work. Dunno jest what I'll do when you'n Miss Kit goes. Pay Dirt won't never be the same, not no more. Dang it all, I spends half last night composin' this here speech uh farewell, then busts down like a bawlin' kid afore I gits off to anywhere near like I start. An' I'll whup the dad-gummed hoot-owl that says I'm chicken-hearted. Dunno how I'll make out, so help me Jupiter, I don't."

Pete led him back to the punch bowl and slipped away.

Pete wanted to be alone. He walked down the deserted street, past the black, charred ruins of Whisky Gulch, past the darkened office of the Pay Dirt *Assay*. Aimlessly, without knowing why, he climbed the mountain hill trail that led to the big flat rock.

Kit had called it her Wishing Rock.

The soft shadows of the tall pines hid its outline. Pete sat down, fumbling for a cigarette. It was then that he found that he was not alone. The faint, elusive scent of perfume. A hushed little sob, out there in the shadows, at the other side of the rock.

"Why, Kitten!" He got to his feet.

"Please go away, Pete! Can't you see I'm all busted up? That I want to be alone?"

"That's exactly why I'll stay, Kitten. I want to be alone just as much as you do. That's why I came up here."

"You mean you didn't see me sneak away and come here, Pete?"

"I did not. This is a public rock. A wishing rock in other

words, placed here for the use of those foolish enough to climb a mile to make a wish that won't come true. Did the darn rock ever get you anything in the way of wishes? Answer me that?"

A moment of silence, then, "Yes."

"When?"

"About five minutes ago."

"Oh. Would it be too much to inquire into the nature of said wish?"

"It would. It would be most rude, Pete Smyth, and impertinent."

"I see."

"But that's the trouble. You don't see. You're dumb."

"Look here, Kathleen Mavourneen Kavanaugh, I won't stand here and be called dumb by anybody. It's been some time since I laid you across my knee and plied the slipper where it did the most good, but still I'm man enough for the job. Dumb? Just because you're the most beautiful, most wonderful, most . . ."

"Go on, Peter, you're doing fine. Most what, dear?"

"Most annoying person I ever saw," finished Pete viciously.

"Gee, Pete," Kit's voice caught a little. "Don't let's spoil such a night. Please come over here and hold my hand and just sit here without saying anything. Maybe, Pete, if we sit here, and not say one word to break the spell, and wish awful hard, Pete, we'll get it." And as Pete came across the big rock, she added, "Isn't it grand, up here?"

"You bet. Wish I didn't have to leave Pay Dirt."

"Wish granted. Why leave, if you like it here?"

Pete did not answer. He sat beside her on the big rock. Kit found his hand and clung to it tightly.

"Now, before we go into this seriously, Pete. I said I made a wish that came true. I was wishing you'd come up here. Not follow me, but just come. And you came."

"Why did you wish that, then. . . ."

"Shhhhh." They sat there for a long time. Above them was the star-filled sky. The perfume of Kit's hair sent Pete's blood pounding. Something of his emotion must have passed through their handclasp into Kit's heart, for she looked up at him, her eyes soft with love, her lips trembling a little. When Pete took her into her arms and kissed her, he knew that his wish had come true. Kit loved him as she had never loved any man.

"Gee . . . dear . . . it worked!"

It was more than an hour later when Pete said, "Almanac will be tickled into D.T.'s when he finds out we're staying here in Pay Dirt."

"Won't he, though?" laughed Kit. "Wish number two. Gosh, Pete, do you think we can get that nice, knock-kneed old parson up this hill to the Wishing Rock?"

"At sunrise, Kit?"

"At sunrise, Pete."

THE END